MAKEUP & MURDER

BEAUTY SECRETS MYSTERY 1

STEPHANIE DAMORE

PINK SAPPHIRE PRESS

Stephanie Damore
Copyright © Stephanie Damore 2017

To Dominic,
who told me I could do it, so I did.

1
_____

*I*n my world, Christmas falls on May 14 every year. That's when the summer issue of *Beauty Secrets* magazine drops, and all my clients anxiously await their copies.

Today was that day.

If the worst part of my job was getting up at sunrise every few months for a couple of catalogs, then I didn't have much to complain about. As soon as those beauties landed on my doorstep, I ripped open the cellophane and dove into the hot new looks of summer. I had seen the product sneak peeks at last month's regional meeting, but was still amazed by all the new fashions. Lipsticks that plumped, mascara that defined, and moisturizers that worked magic, rounded the lineup. Sexy summer skin was merely a click away. Out with the smoky eye shadows and heavy bronzers. In with soft watercolors for the eyes, shimmering blushes, and bright nail polishes—the *romantic* look. I was eager to try it out, and I was certain my clients would flip for it too.

I knew I'd have to be on my A-game if I was to visit all of them before sunset, which is why I was steering my little

Chevy pickup truck down Sugar Plantation by a quarter after eight, toward my first client's house. Yes, I know it's not the sexiest of rides; but hey, it was free—thanks to my parents—and no car payment meant extra money for shopping. *Hello, Nordstrom!*

My first stop was to see Aria, my best friend, and the first one to snatch up any free samples. Thankfully, she also hosted the best parties, so I didn't mind. Aria's a girl's girl—fashionably chic and a straight-talker with a sweet spot for nail polish. Her love of the candy-colored lacquer made her a platinum-card-carrying, top-notch client for Beauty Secrets, and the new summer shade selection promised to deliver. I had the free samples to prove it.

I pulled into Aria's neighborhood and gagged at the bubble-gum colored Jeep idling at the stop sign waiting to pull out. What was Justine Martin doing here? The woman was my arch enemy ever since fourth and a new beauty representative for that *Other Company*, a fact that I wasn't able to understand given that her makeup looked like she slapped it on with a paint brush. If pastels were in, I'd guarantee her face looked like a chalked up Easter egg. It was no coincidence she was pulling out of my business' most popular neighborhood the day of a catalog drop. I knew better.

She rolled down her window and leaned forward as I slowed to turn in. Her fluffy white poodle sat on the seat next to her wearing some ridiculous sequined outfit. The poor pup. I sped up as I turned the corner instead. My truck splashed some nice muddy water off the road curtesy of the last night's rain onto her gaudy ride. I smiled at her shocked expression and gave her a little wave. I hadn't willingly spoken to her since 1995. I didn't see any reason for that to change today.

When I pulled into Aria's driveway, her front door was already open and her son Arjun stood there in his monster pajamas, action figures in hand, being the look out. He smooshed his face against the glass when he saw me, complete with blown-out cheeks and finger antlers. I laughed, and he took off racing down the hall like a wild child—a characteristic I know he picked up from his mother. While she has definitely mellowed out in her thirties, get a couple tequila shots in her and she's nineteen again. Girls' nights are always an adventure.

A second later, Aria came to the door, looking as much like a fashionista as ever. She could make even yoga pants look glamorous, which she did almost every day at the downtown fitness studio where she taught.

I waved hello and bent down to grab my client binder, aka my *Beauty Bible*. I never made a house call without it. The binder was key to my success in the business. It held record of every product my clients purchased, along with a register that included the date, item numbers, and methods of payment. My beauty business would be a mess without it.

"What's up, girlie?" Aria asked, opening the front door.

Before I could answer, Arjun came zipping back down the hall, sporting a pair of red rain boots and a cowboy hat, ready to head out the front door.

"Excuse me, little man. Where do you think you're going?" Aria asked.

"Outside," replied Arjun, trying to wrangle past his mom.

"I don't think so. You know the rules," Aria replied.

"Ooohhhh!" Arjun's little fists got all tight and his cheeks puckered in as he wound up to pitch a preschooler's fit. I knew where this was headed if Aria didn't calm him down quickly.

"Give me twenty minutes with Aunt Ziva, and then we'll go out together. Got it?" Aria said.

I loved it when Aria referred to me as Aunt Ziva. We weren't really sisters, but we were the closest thing to it for each other.

Aria shut the front door, putting an end to the matter. Arjun stomped his rubber boots and did an about-face and headed to the living room. The clamor of engines roaring and monster trucks being dumped out onto the hardwood floor, soon followed. Disaster adverted for now.

"No seriously, what's up? You look ticked." Aria knew me well.

"Justine," I said, and shuddered. "She wasn't here, was she?"

"Girl, did you bump your head? You honestly think she'd stop by my house?"

Back in grade school, when Justine turned all my girl-friends against me, making my world seem very small, Aria was the only one who stood by my side. She was still there today.

"I passed her on my way in. I know she's up to some-thing. She always is," I said.

"Pshhh, let her try. She's pathetic. Latte?"

"With soy?" It was a rhetorical question. With Aria, it was always with soy milk or almond milk, or whatever milk alternative she had in her fridge.

"You know it," she replied.

"Pass." Nothing ruined a good latte like soy milk. Gross. I took my lattes with two percent at least, whole milk prefer-ably, and skip the coffee. I was chai all the way.

"A little bit of good nutrition wouldn't kill you. Did you get in your run this morning?"

Aria knew I tried to work out a least a couple times a

week to make up for my poor eating habits. Okay, make that downright horrible eating habits, but business had been booming and exercise was at the bottom of my to-do list.

I couldn't hide my guilt. "Yeah, of course."

"Liar." Aria didn't even have to look up to know that I was full of it.

I laughed. "But hey, at least my jeans still fit." Although, at that moment, my jeans did feel a little tight. They were a denim-spandex fabric too. *Maybe I should just switch to leggings. Those are quite fashionable nowadays, and a good beauty consultant is always in style.*

"You mean *my* jeans?" said Aria.

"Aren't those *my* heels by the door?" I asked.

Aria met me with a coy smile. It was a fair trade and she knew it. It seemed both of our closets had revolving doors. We couldn't keep track of who borrowed what.

"Speaking of fashion, did you hear that Winston's was robbed last night?"

Winston's was an upscale fashion boutique located downtown on the waterfront. It was Aria's and my go-to shop for accessories like designer sunglasses and leather handbags.

"What? No way. That's like the second break-in this week. Didn't someone just hit up the yacht club?" I asked.

"Yeah, made off with the charity gala proceeds too."

"What? I didn't know that. Who would steal from a charity?"

"Not a clue, but there are a couple purses at Winston's I'd like to get my hands on too," Aria said.

"I know, right?"

I could drop a small fortune in that store if I wasn't careful. It was actually after one particularly pricey shopping spree, which ended there, that I decided I would be a cash-only customer from that point forward. No cash meant no shopping. It was a tough rule, but I stuck to it. My credit score thanked me.

"Is that it?" Aria changed the subject in a hot second when she spotted my client binder on the table.

I smiled and slid the catalog out of the front cover. "Here you go. I don't understand why you even need to look. You know you're going to order the entire line."

"Oh, shut up and give it to me." Aria opened the catalog directly to the nail polish page and fell in love. "Oh, girlie, look at this one. Atomic Sun? It's bright and citrusy. I love it, love it, love it. Oh, and these pinks are perfect. I have to have them," she said.

"Told you," I replied.

Over the next half hour, I proceeded to mark Aria down for all thirteen new shades, one for each week of summer, and I was confident she'd wear every one of them. I completed Aria's order, detached the yellow carbon receipt for her records, and filed the white copy in my client binder with the rest of the orders I planned on processing the next morning.

My cell phone rang in my purse while we were wrapping up, and I didn't need to look at it to know that it was Mrs. Birdie Jackson, aka Mrs. J., calling to hound me for being late. Having three Beauty Secrets clients in the same plantation saved time making deliveries, but it also meant you couldn't socialize at one house for too long. Mrs. J. seemed to always know when I was in the neighborhood, and patience wasn't a virtue she was blessed with.

Mrs. J. was sitting on her front porch, waiting impatiently

for me to arrive. She started in with me before I even shut the car door.

"You know, this jam cake's been sitting outside here for almost an hour? I can't keep the sun from drying it out all day." She motioned to the large slice of strawberry cake and tall glass of lemonade sitting beside her on the front porch breakfast table. Bless Mrs. J. I loved Aria, but a girl needs her sweets. How she survived on carrot sticks and humus was beyond me. What was humus anyway?

I doubted Mrs. J. had been sitting out there for an hour, but I didn't say anything. The whole town of Port Haven knew not to make Mrs. J. mad, unless you didn't like your reputation, or her cooking. You see, Mrs. Birdie Jackson was known for three things—her crazy sense of fashion, her love of gossip, and her amazing baking skills. Today, she was wearing a lime green suit and a matching white hat with lime green polka-dot trim. The bright color perfectly complimented her shiny red nails and matching lipstick. Only a rich southern woman could pull this look off and, believe me, Mrs. J. could. She had a style and a bank account that more than a few women in the neighborhood envied. Back in the day, Mrs. J. and my Nan were the best of friends. Those two ladies were the eyes and ears of Port Haven. You couldn't step a toe out of line without them getting word of it, and knowing what you stepped in, too. My Nan had since passed on, but Mrs. J. kept the tradition alive.

"Morning, Mrs. J."

"Morning? Sug', it's almost noon."

No, it wasn't. I had another hour before she could make that claim, not that it mattered. I looked down on her table and saw Justine's card with a sample lipstick and her own company's catalog. My heart sank. Not only had Justine beaten me there, but I had left Mrs. J.'s Passion Pout lipstick at home. *My day started out so well.*

"Mmm-hmm. At least someone can get out of bed before noon." I knew what Mrs. J. was implying. Justine was an early riser. She had probably gone to the gym this morning too. Oh, how I hated her.

"I know, I know, but Justine doesn't love you like I do," I said with a smile. "Besides, today was a little extra crazy with the new catalog drop and all." I sensed Mrs. J. wanted more details, but all she got was, "I had to stop by Aria's first."

"That girl's still in town?" I ignored Mrs. J.'s rhetorical question. "I would have bet all the cornbread in Savannah that she'd hightail it straight back to India after Raja died last spring."

"Aria's from Atlanta," I remarked. "And Raja passed away two years ago."

Mrs. J. didn't acknowledge my comments. "You know how those young girls are, always looking for an old man with money. I could've spotted her shovel from a Mississippi-mile away."

This wasn't the first time Mrs. J. had called Aria a gold digger, but I didn't believe it. Aria wasn't the money-grubbing type. Although, even I had to admit her late husband, Raja Patal, wasn't much of a looker. Add that to their thirty-year age difference and Aria's beauty, and I could see how someone could make the case.

I was still thinking about Aria and Raja when Mrs. J. said, "Did you hear? Someone broke into Winston's last night. Patsy Ann told me all about it this morning at the Piggly Wiggly."

Being friends with Patsy Ann pretty much eliminated

the need for a police scanner. Her husband was a local deputy and told her everything.

"I know, I heard. I love that store," I said.

"Who doesn't? It sounds like the crook made off with a pretty paycheck too. At least that's what her husband said. I tell you, this town is just swirling right down the drain."

I agreed with Mrs. J. Port Haven was definitely changing, and it wasn't for the better.

"Tell me you got something to cheer me up, sug'. I could sure use a reason to smile." Mrs. J. looked downright depressed.

I opened my binder and handed her a new catalog, along with a couple extra free samples I knew she'd love, to remind her why *I* was the best. It worked. Mrs. J.'s face lit up. In that moment, I was reminded of why I loved my job so much. Somewhere during our visit, I mumbled something about her lipstick not being in yet (a flat out lie, I know), but Mrs. J. didn't care. She pushed the jam cake my way and let the world of Beauty Secrets float her cares away.

2

*G*ood thing I can set my own schedule because, if I had a boss, I'd be fired by now. My beauty consultant butt should've high tailed it out of Mrs. J.'s an hour earlier but, nope, I had to have a second serving of jam cake and get wrapped up in the gossip. Not that I ever said anything. That'd be a big Beauty Secrets no-no, but that didn't mean I couldn't be entertained. It's just a fact that no visit to Mrs. J.'s was ever quick, and some days it was harder to leave than others. I would've socialized another hour away if I hadn't remembered I wanted to talk to Marion about hosting another party. The last party she hosted had been a major success, earning me Consultant of the Month, and a couple new clients to boot. The new summer promos surely would tempt her into hosting again. At least I hoped so.

The Siebold house was just off Palmetto Court toward the back of the plantation. To me, it was a smart place to build a house, away from the golfers. I always thought it was crazy for people to place their houses smack-dab on the fairway, like a target waiting to be whacked by a golf ball. If you were lucky, and your house didn't get hit, you still had to deal with strangers trampling all over your property. What a waste.

The Siebolds didn't have that problem. Sheltered by deep overhangs and a wraparound porch, their house was a fine example of Southern living. I adored that wraparound porch. Mrs. J. called them sipping porches because you could sip an afternoon away on them. I wasn't so sure about that, but I never objected to sipping a glass of sweet tea or swinging on the Seiebolds' porch swing while talking shop. But the closed-up nature of the house told me there wouldn't be any sipping today and, honestly, that was fine by me. I'd already had enough sweets to sweat off after my visit with Mrs. J. I just hoped Marion was home. It wasn't like her to be out when she knew I'd be stopping over, especially on a day when I had the new catalog and her product order to deliver, but the closed blinds didn't offer me much hope. Of course, it wasn't a huge deal if she was out. Like with all my clients, Marion and I had arranged a designated delivery drop-off spot, but no Marion meant no booked party, and I'd have to make another house call later in the week.

I gathered my client binder and Marion's beauty-filled gift bag off the passenger seat, and bumped the car door closed with my hip. It shut with a hard thud. I was definitely getting a little extra junk in my trunk. *Looks like I'd better add ten more minutes to tomorrow's run … and get those leggings sooner rather than later.*

Even though the house looked empty, I took a chance and headed to the front door first. One of Justine's cards was slid in by the handle. I took the pink, glittery card out and read it. The woman was actually offering a twenty-five percent discount to all existing Beauty Secrets' clients who booked with her this month. I couldn't believe it. Justine was actively trying to steal my clients. She was nuts if she thought I was going to sit back and let her take away my business. Enough women lived in Port Haven for us both to have successful businesses, but Justine never thought that way. I wanted to rip her stupid card into tiny pieces or light it on fire, but instead slipped it into my back pocket to deal with later.

I rang Marion's door bell and stepped back in anticipation of Charlie's incessant barking. The silver Weimaraner was hyper, to say the least. He'd knocked my heels out from under me a time or two and slobbered on more than one pair of designer jeans. I'd learned my lesson.

But all was silent.

Marion was out, and she must have taken Charlie with her.

With gift bag in tow, I stepped off the porch and followed the slate walkway around back to the sunroom. I punched my code into the automatic keypad and waited for the door lock to release. Sliding the heavy glass door down the metal track, I stepped inside. Even with the door open, the room felt warm and stuffy. Sweat beaded on my brow, and I wiped it away with my hand while surveying the room. The sunroom was all Marion. A white velvet chaise lounge ran alongside a wall of windows, her home-designer magazines tucked neatly in a rack beside it. Two slipper chairs with bold, blue floral print created a cozy seating area in the far-right corner. Deep blue accent pillows contrasted with the rest of the white accents and cream-colored carpeted floor. A potted lemon tree sat in a beautiful blue ceramic pot in the corner. Marion loved when her tree would flower and she could have fresh lemons for her afternoon tea, but even her lovely tree looked a bit droopy in the heat. I assumed Marion's air conditioner was on the fritz again. It went out last year at the end of a brutal Southern heat wave and seemed to act up every now again. That probably explained why she and Charlie were out. I wouldn't stay in this sweat box if I could help it. I couldn't leave her product in here either. Melted lipstick did no one any good.

I turned around to walk back out and caught myself off balance. I didn't know if it was the heat of the room or a reaction to all the sugar I'd eaten, but I felt queasy. I sat down to steady myself. The room wasn't spinning, but my mouth was parched. Maybe a glass of water would help to flush the sugar out of my system and make me feel a little more normal. *I'd hate to have a dizzy spell overcome me while driving.*

I stood up and headed toward Marion's kitchen, intending to grab a bottle of water and drink it outside where the air was cooler, but something on the kitchen floor stopped me. It looked like Marion had stenciled a mosaic pattern onto her hardwood floor. An ugly mosaic pattern. *What in the world?* I hated to think it, but it reminded me of a home-show segment gone wrong. Marion needed to lay off the home-designer shows. Some things should be left to the professionals.

But when I looked again, I realized I was wrong. Stencils didn't smear, not like that.

"Sweet sugar!" They weren't stencils at all, but bloody paw prints, dozens of them all down the foyer! That explained why Marion and Charlie were gone. Poor pup, he must have cut his paw on something. On what, I had no idea. I looked around for a clue and a dish cloth. The least I could do was clean this mess up.

I walked to the sink and began wetting a washcloth, and that's when I heard the growl. It wasn't a warning, but the feral sound an animal makes before it attacks. I turned to see Charlie behind me. Congealed blood matted his silver coat and muzzle. Gone was the playful pup, only to be replaced by a wild animal. I had never been afraid of that dog until that moment.

My feet fumbled a few steps backwards toward the door. Making my voice as soothing as possible, I said, "Charlie, it's okay. Calm down boy." Getting worked up wouldn't help the situation. I didn't want to hurt the dog, but I needed to find a weapon in case he attacked. For all I knew, the blood on the floor and his coat wasn't his own. Maybe Charlie was a mind reader because he wasn't buying my act, no matter how soft I spoke to him.

Charlie crouched back on his hindquarters, lips barred, daring me to move. I had no idea what had happened here, but I was in trouble.

With my full attention on Charlie, I didn't realize someone had snuck up behind me until the man's forearm rounded my neck and locked me in place. My wide eyes locked with Charlie's. It took a second for my mind to catch up and tell my body to fight back. I dropped my binder and reached for the man's arm, gripping his wrist to pull myself free. Charlie circled around us, barking and snapping. At first, I wasn't sure whose side he was on.

I dug my nails into the man's skin, hoping to cause enough pain for him to let go, but that only encouraged him to squeeze harder. One slight movement of my neck and I feared it would snap. My head swam and my lips started to tingle as I gasped for air. Charlie lunged for the man, but he was quicker and kicked the dog before it could bite. Charlie slid across the floor, visibly hurt. If only I could kick this guy. *These heels could do some damage.* I stomped on his foot and elbowed him at the same time, but I was too weak to cause any real harm. Everything around me went black.

MARION's hysterical screams pulled me back into the moment. Let me tell you, that's one heck of a way to wake up. Charlie pranced around me and licked my face as I came to. His blood-stained snout nuzzled my neck, leaving a trail of sticky slobber. The beast was gone and the pup had returned, visibly concerned for my safety.

Quick inventory told me that I was fine, except for the raging headache that had started to build behind my eyes, and the dried blood on my arms and shorts from where I slid onto the floor. Sirens pulled into the driveway before I could even get up to find Marion. Her sobs echoed throughout the house in total madness. On cue, Charlie's insistent yaps and yowls added to the mayhem. Confusion wasn't my favorite state of mind and, right now, I was utterly bewildered.

When the officers knocked on the door, it felt like they were pounding inside my head as I got up to answer it.

"Ma'am, are you all right?" Officer A asked immediately upon assessing my appearance. Officer B didn't wait for my answer. He was already calling for backup.

I shook my head yes, which increased my dizziness, as I opened the door further. Charlie came to the door to investigate. His bloodied appearance did little to clarify the situation. The officers froze, and I could only wonder what carnage they expected to find inside.

Marion walked into the foyer, interrupting the scene, cell phone clutched in her hand. "Oh, thank you," she said when she saw me. "Not you too. Roger—" she pointed toward the family room and started shaking. I swear she was about to collapse. Marion's a petite little thing; I could've easily supported her weight, but I didn't have to. Officer A came to her rescue and led her over to the stairwell to sit, while Officer B went into the family room with his gun at the ready.

I wanted to sneak out the front door and run away, to put whatever the hell just happened in there behind me. Instead, I pulled on my big girl panties and allowed Officer A to escort me out to the front porch, where I sat on the cement steps while he attended to Marion. More officers arrived—maybe a detective or two—crime scene tape went up, and a news vans pulled in as I sat there for a long while, waiting for my turn to talk. Officer A came over and took down my contact information somewhere along the way. Maybe he was afraid that I would bolt. I reassured him that I wasn't going anywhere, and he told me that my turn with the detective was next. Another officer showed up beside me a moment later and just stood there, keeping an eye on me.

While I waited to be interviewed, a paramedic also came over for an assessment, which I assured him wasn't necessary. I must've looked like hell because he didn't believe me. I let him give me a once over, but refused when he suggested I take a ride with him to the hospital. My insurance didn't cover ambulance rides, and I didn't need to tackle on a hospital bill to boot. The paramedic finally relented when I joked that I was going for a new look—horror chick—and I promised to follow up with my doctor in the next day or so.

The paramedic left at about the same time I spotted Mrs. J., bobbing down the street in a half walk, half run. The excitement was just too much for her to wait to go through the normal gossip channels. Officer A stopped her from walking up the driveway, to which she replied, "Don't you ma'am me, Peter Whitemore. I taught you in Sunday school, and I know your grandmother. Now you tell me who's being wheeled out there." Mrs. J. motioned toward the body bag being loaded onto the ambulance. I, for one, was trying to look anywhere other than at the gurney, but not Mrs. J. You'd think she had x-ray vision the way she scrutinized that bag. The moment she saw me, her eyes lit up like the Fourth of July. I could count the seconds until she'd be ringing up my cell phone.

A man in his mid-forties came out of the house and headed in my direction. His hair was neat, dark blonde with a little gray. The black dress pants he wore were clean, and his white Oxford button-down shirt still had the creases in it from the package. His posture and appearance gave him an earnest, hardworking sort of look. He reminded me of my dad.

"Hello, Ms. Diaz. I'm Detective Brandle," he said, his hand extended.

I got up and shook it, turning my back on Mrs. J., even though I was sure she wasn't going anywhere.

"What can you tell me about what happened in there?" he asked.

I recounted the morning's events, recalling every detail from the warmth of the sunroom to the bloody paw prints on the kitchen floor, and the attacker's strong choke hold. I knew I was rambling, but I couldn't stop. Detective Brandle's cell phone rang a half a dozen times during the interview. On the sixth time, he finally interrupted me to answer it. Usually, I'm good about my manners and don't eavesdrop (a good rule of thumb for any beauty consultant), but Detective Brandle's voice carried, so I listened.

"Send Jones... Why not?" Inaudible grumble. "No, that's fine. What time? ... I'll see what I can do." The detective stuffed his cell phone back in his pocket and looked at his watch. I knew an overworked man when I saw one, and my rambling wasn't helping.

"Listen, I know you're pressed for time," I said, "so let me summarize this for you. I came into the house, went for a drink of water, saw the blood, Charlie growled at me, and then I was attacked. I have no idea who attacked me, and I can't even describe him. I never saw his face, and he never said a word. About the only thing I can tell you is that he had dark arm hair and smelled of Midnight."

"Midnight?"

"You know, the cologne? My ex used to wear it." *Where did that come from?* It's weird how you remember details like that. I could still smell the scent on my clothes.

"Height? Build?" Detective Brandle's pen was at the ready.

"He was taller than me, but I'm only five-one, so that's not saying much." I like to think I'm a tough cookie, but he overpowered me with no problem.

"The paramedics said you're okay. Are you sure you don't need any medical attention?" he asked.

"No, I'm good." My neck was sore, but it was nothing that an ibuprofen and a change of clothes couldn't cure. Maybe with a chocolate martini on the side.

The detective took a closer look. "Your neck's already bruising. You're going to want to ice that," he said.

"Got it," I said.

"Here's my card. Call me if you think of anything else. Is this your correct contact information?" The detective read back the address and phone number I'd given Officer Whitmore earlier. I told him it was. "Good. I'll be in touch if I have any other questions."

That was fine by me.

With the detective gone, I assumed I was free to go. Although, one look at the cars parked behind my pickup told me I wouldn't be driving off in it anytime soon.

No one paid much attention to me as I went over to the truck to fetch my cell phone. Mrs. J. might have left, but she wasn't giving up. I already had eleven missed phone calls, eight from Mrs. J. The other three were from Aria, exactly who I wanted to talk to. She answered before the first ring and said she already had her car keys in hand and was on her way out the door. *I chose well in the best-friend department.*

I spotted Marion while waiting for Aria to come get me. She was standing on the side of the house talking with Detective Brandle. But it was the man standing next to her who had my attention. I didn't know who he was, but boy did he know how to dress. *Yowza!* He was wearing gray, pin-striped dress pants with a baby blue dress shirt. The sleeves had been rolled about a quarter of the way up his arm. I suddenly felt very self-conscious in my blood-stained shorts. Good thing he was too occupied consoling Marion to notice me. Had it not been for me looking like a hot mess, I would've gone over and introduced myself. As that wasn't the case, I continued to study him from afar. The guy couldn't have been much older than me, maybe in his late-thirties; yet, the way he carried himself reminded me of someone much older. Maybe it was the way he dressed. Men in business attire always seemed more mature, but I doubted it was that lone detail that stood out. My eyes studied him for a minute longer. I couldn't place my finger on it, but the moment Aria pulled up, I no longer cared. I was more than ready to get out of there. Not wanting to seem like I was running away, I checked out with Officer Whitemore before jumping into Aria's car and taking off. Relief washed over me as the Siebold house faded in the rearview mirror, even if we were just going around the block.

3

---

*W*hen your world goes to hell, you need two things: 1. Your best friend. 2. Chocolate. I would've called my mom (better she heard it from me than Mrs. J.), but she and Dad were on a private Mediterranean cruise, celebrating their fortieth anniversary. My mom put the P in proper. You would've too if your mother had been my Nan. My mom wasn't able to get away with a thing when she was a kid, without my grandma finding out. As a result, she was a little too straight-laced for my taste, but she was still my mom. She would've been horrified to hear what had happened to me, but I knew she would've gotten over it fast and taken care of everything. I liked to think of her as my PR manager. But I couldn't call her. I didn't want to ruin their trip, and I knew Mom would drag Dad to the nearest airport for the next flight home as soon as their ship docked, no matter how much I objected. I couldn't do that to them. Mom had been planning this trip for months, and they deserved this once-in-a-lifetime vacation.

Aria was the best person to talk to, anyway. She could keep her cool and would let me finish my story without drowning me in questions, which was what I needed. Someone to just listen. That and, health junky or not, Aria was bound to have chocolate in her house somewhere. Another reason why she was my best friend.

After filling Aria in as to what happened, and gorging myself on her dark chocolate stash (she swore it was healthier), I took a hot shower and a nap. It was the best nap of my life. Only once did I wake, and that was to the ringing of the doorbell. Somehow, Mrs. J. tracked me down and was begging Aria to let her talk with me. From what I gathered, Mrs. J. had even brought a cake. While the dessert was tempting, I pulled the covers over my head and prayed Aria would get rid of her. I could hear Mrs. J. insisting that she see me just to make sure I was okay, and that was the least she could do for my Nan, "God rest her soul." Aria must have convinced her of my safety because I fell back asleep and didn't wake again until morning.

The house seemed empty when I woke. I lay motionless and listened to the silence. Sunlight glinted through the blinds and cast dancing shadows on the bedspread and walls. I was content to lie there and watch them. It was my only moment of peace before the memories of yesterday crept back in. The shock of it all had finally set in. The moment my mind started reeling, I was compelled to get up. Realizing that I could've been killed—or worse—yesterday, wasn't sitting well with me. I couldn't afford to sit around and feel like a victim. I said a quick prayer to my Nan for covering me, and got my butt out of bed. No sense in lying around thinking about what could've happened. I needed a good workout, and still had a handful of clients to touch base with. Plus, I wanted to check in with Detective Brandle. I doubt he had any news, but even hearing nothing was something.

Aria's kitchen contained the usual rabbit fare—that is, nothing I would eat—along with a note, saying she was teaching a morning class but would be back around noon. Aria's classes were packed because she was a yoga goddess. Seriously, she could bend and twist her body into positions that weren't natural. And she didn't mind showing off her mad skills.

Breakfast was almost a wash until I spotted the double-fudge cake that Mrs. J. had dropped off the day before. Had I known that's what she'd baked, I might have changed my mind and come out to chat for a bit. The cake was *that* good, famous in these parts. I wondered, on more than one occasion, what she put into it to make it so rich, but I eventually decided I didn't care, and simply devoured it. In fact, Mrs. J. made the cake for my engagement party. Looking back, it would've been more satisfying to date the cake than my ex-fiancé.

The cake had sat untouched on Aria's counter. How she'd resisted the temptation was beyond me. I pulled the plastic wrap off and helped myself to a double-wide slice. It was pure heaven. My lips tingled from the sugar and I felt giddy. I hate to say it, but I inhaled that cake. I would've licked the plate too had I not scraped every smudge of frosting off with my fork. It wasn't long before a second slice was calling me, and I knew I needed to get out of the house before I caved in.

With my hair in a ponytail and Aria's workout clothes on my back, I locked up the house and headed out toward Marion's. It had been too many days since I worked out, and a run would give me a chance to work off some of my cake guilt. Well, that, and I wanted to retrieve the pickup and my *Beauty Bible*. I prayed the police hadn't confiscated either for evidence. I didn't think they would, but what did I know?

My knowledge of police protocol was limited to network television.

I set off at a fast-paced walk, just enough to warm up my muscles. It wasn't long before I kicked the pace up to a jog, and my breathing fell into its usual rhythm: inhale two paces, exhale two paces, repeat. I never ran without music. The process was painful enough with my jams urging me on but, today, my thoughts proved to be distracting enough. I thought about Marion and wondered how she was holding up. I should have called first instead of showing up unannounced. I was already halfway there, though, and wasn't about to pull out my cell phone mid-run. Chances were, she wasn't even home. I wouldn't blame her either. For all I knew, the house was a crime scene and she wasn't even allowed to enter. I prayed that I was wrong because, if that was the case, who knew when I'd get my *Beauty Bible* back. At least I should be able to pick up my little truck. Although, given the choice, I'd rather have my binder back any day.

Turned out, someone *was* home. Rounding onto Palmetto Court, I slowed my pace at the sight of a black car in the Siebolds' driveway. I had the fleeting thought that maybe Detective Brandle was there paying a visit, until I saw that the car was a Rolls Royce. No chance the detective made that kind of bank. Approaching the house, I saw that I was right. It wasn't Detective Brandle at all, rather, the mysterious man from yesterday. He stood on the front porch, dressed much the same as the day before, with a black suit and coordinating gray dress shirt and silver tie. Yesterday had not been a fluke. The man had style. He also seemed to be amused. It took me a minute to understand why, until Marion came into view. She was zigzagging across the front yard, almost in a run, picking up what looked like sticks. The man shook his head in an exasperated gesture when he spotted me. Marion turned to see who he was looking at and saw me walking up the driveway.

"Ziva, so glad you stopped by," she said when I reached her. "I've been thinking about you all night. I was just telling Eric we had to get your truck back over to you, and I wanted to check and see how you were doing. How are you feeling?" Marion said all of this while continuing her mission to rid the yard of every twig she could find. Her face had a fresh peachy glow to it that I knew was part perspiration part Just Kissed tinted moisturizing cream.

I wanted to tell her I'd feel better if she'd stand still for a minute. My neck was sore from following her around the yard but, because I knew that wasn't going to happen, I said, "I'm all right. How about you?"

Marion didn't answer or stop moving. Instead, she said, "Oh, where are my manners? Ziva, this is Roger's business partner, Eric Pérez." *So, the mystery man has a name.* It suited him.

Eric walked over to greet me. "Nice to meet you," he said, extending his hand. Eric's words were reflected in his eyes, and I could tell he was being sincere. It took me a moment to find my manners. After all, how could this man be Roger's business partner? Eric looked far too young to be a seasoned investment banker. That explained the mature vibe I got from him. "Are you sure you're okay? I wanted to ask yesterday, but you left before I had a chance," he said.

"Yeah, I'm okay, really." I resisted the urge to rub my neck. The bruises hadn't gotten any worse, and my darker skin tone hid them well. Eric and I continued to watch Marion. I didn't know what she was going to do when she picked up all the sticks, but doubted she planned to sit down.

I took advantage of Marion being occupied to ask Eric

what happened yesterday. I hadn't heard any details, and I was curious.

"No one told you?" he asked.

I shook my head no. "I've tuned out the world the last twenty-four hours," I explained.

"Roger was murdered. Someone stabbed him right in the heart." Eric pointed to his chest.

I was speechless.

"I know, and it gets worse. The police said he probably knew the guy," he replied.

"What? Why? Why would they say that?" I asked.

"Because nothing was stolen or broken. So, it doesn't sound like a robbery, or like Roger saw it coming," Eric supplied.

"I can't even imagine..." I hugged myself and tried to focus on the fact that I was safe. I didn't want to acknowledge what *could've* happened. Seemed like I got off light with the choke hold. Yet another reason why Roger's murder was probably personal and not random. The killer hadn't wanted anything to do with me, not really. That's what I was hoping for anyway.

Marion tossed the sticks into a pile by the porch and then went about picking up pinecones. In no time, her hands were full. I watched in amazement. I whispered to Eric, "Has she been like this all morning?"

"She hasn't stopped for a second. I wanted her to take a break, but she won't. The landscapers won't know what to when they get here tomorrow," he said.

"Eric, what was the name of that cleaning company? The one Detective Brandle said handled messes like this? He never called with the number," Marion hollered across the yard. It took me a second to realize the mess she was referring to wasn't her overpopulation of pinecones, but rather the blood stains, and who only knew what else, that was inside the house.

"I'm not sure. I'll check with him and schedule an appointment," replied Eric.

"Good, good. That's one less thing I have to do. See if they can come this afternoon. I should be back from the dry cleaner by one," Marion said.

"She's having Roger's suit dry cleaned," Eric explained. I must have looked confused. "For the funeral," he added. I doubted Roger cared if he was buried in a clean suit or not, but I kept my mouth shut on the matter.

"Have you heard from the detective?" I asked Eric.

"No, I've left him a message though. I'm hoping he'll call back soon," he said.

Marion interrupted us. "Actually, make it three. After the dry cleaner's, I'm running to the bank and then the attorney's office, and hopefully over to the funeral home." Marion carried on and on. Sooner or later, she was going to crash with the weight of reality; but, until then, she wasn't slowing down.

"Marion, it's Sunday. The bank and attorney's offices are closed," Eric replied, but I don't think she heard him.

"What about the alarm company? What time are they coming over? I want to upgrade the system as soon as possible," she continued.

"Not until tomorrow morning. Is that okay? Do you want me to stay tonight?" Eric asked.

"Good heavens, no. I'll be fine." Marion started adding pine needles to the pile. This could take a while, seeing how the perimeter of the yard was lined with pine trees. With her head to the ground, she added, "Ziva, you left your binder here. It's inside on the kitchen table. Eric, go inside and get it for her."

I could've gone and gotten it, but Eric was already to the door and made his way in and out in a matter of minutes, with my binder in hand. "Here you go." "Detective Brandle said it was in the clear zone, so it's free to be moved."

"Sweet. You have no idea how important this binder is to me. I really need to back it up somehow," I said.

"You don't keep electronic files?" Eric asked.

"Not of everything," I said.

"Do you want help with that?" he asked.

"How so?" I didn't see how he could digitalize my *Beauty Bible*.

"I have a scanner that reads documents and exports them as computer files. Bring your binder by the office next week, and I can help you with it," he said.

"Really? Does it just turn them into PDFs?" I wasn't sure how helpful that would be.

"No, you can do all sorts of things—create client profiles, generate invoices, even email receipts. We use it all the time at the office," he said.

"Oh yeah, for sure then. I'm definitely interested."

"Great. Just give the office a call and my secretary will set something up."

"Awesome, thanks."

"What do you need help with?" Marion asked, joining us on the porch.

"Oh nothing, just talking business." Marion didn't even listen to my response. I had no idea what she was thinking at that moment, but it wasn't about me or Eric. She was zoned out.

"Marion, are you okay?" Eric asked.

"Me? Oh yes, fine, fine. Now what was I just going to do? Oh, that's right, get freshened up to head into town. If you two don't mind, I've got a million things to do." Marion turned and walked away from us. Eric and I both looked at each other, and I shrugged my shoulders. Whatever Eric might have been planning on saying to Marion, he didn't. Instead, he told her to call him if she needed anything. Marion didn't even acknowledge him. If fact, she didn't even wait for us to get to our cars before heading inside and shutting the door. Maybe exhaustion had finally set in, or maybe she needed a moment to herself. Whatever the reason, she clearly wanted us to leave, and who were we to argue? It was fine by me. I had my truck and my Bible, and I was ready to continue my day. As much as I wished my ten-minute jog had cut it, I knew I still had a run to finish up, and I knew the perfect spot.

I CHANGED my mind about running as soon as I reached the marina. It was usually cooler by the water, but not today. There wasn't an ocean breeze to be felt. Puerto Rican genes or not, the sun had turned brutal, and suffering from heat stroke wouldn't do me any good. I couldn't justify abandoning my workout efforts entirely, though, not when I was already dressed for it and knew how much my body needed it. Aria was always going on about my body being a temple and all that. I rolled my eyes at the thought, but it stuck with me nevertheless. If her voice was going to be rolling around in my head, I might as well put it to good use, which is why I headed down to the waterfront to get in some yoga. I didn't have a mat in the car, but I knew there was a beach towel tossed in the cab somewhere. I kicked off my shoes and socks, and walked barefoot through the grass—towel in hand—toward the water's edge. A large-leaf palm tree provided the ample shade I needed.

There's a reason workout DVDs are filmed at the beach: the setting is perfect. The beauty of the water and the charm of the marina always put me in the right state of mind. Waves lapped up and retreated in a perfect rhythm, and I found myself breathing with the steady cadence. Here, it was easy to block out the ringing of my cell phone nearby and the memories of yesterday. Mind relaxed, I stretched out my body and focused my breaths with each movement. Inhale, reach up. Exhale, stretch out. Eyes closed, I held each pose as a couple waves rushed on shore, before moving onto the next.

My workout was going so well, until I opened my eyes and spotted a guy I had dubbed *the shirtless hottie,* wearing only cargo shorts and a red bandana, working on a boat nearby. I swear, the man never wore a shirt. Not that I'm complaining. It's just, it does make it a bit of challenge to be all Zen-like when you have a guy like that in your field of vision.

I watched as the shirtless hottie bent down and then regain his height, taking a swig off a can of Coke. I licked my parched lips, noting my own thirst in that moment. My arms stopped mid-stretch, as if someone had paused my workout DVD. The hottie's southern summer tan and lean body frame had caught my attention on more than one occasion. I could've admired him for hours. Something about him just oozed boy-next-door charm. Good looking, hardworking, you know the type. I wanted him to be *my* neighbor.

It took some serious self-control, but I managed to stop thinking about the hottie long enough to get in five more minutes of my workout. By the time my cell phone rang, I was ready to call it good. I walked over to my bag to see who was calling. I hoped it was Detective Brandle with some good news. Something along the lines of "*Guess what? We caught the killer. Your nightmare is over!"* would be nice. But it wasn't him. It was Maggie, the manager at my parents' condo. Her name sent a jolt down to my toes. I knew exactly why she was calling, without even answering. I had scheduled a beauty demo at the condo clubhouse weeks before, and had completely forgotten about it. *Sweet sugar.* It's not like I could cancel it now, even if I was totally unprepared. Clients drop like flies if they even suspect you're unreliable, and I knew Justine would be right there to scoop them up. I couldn't have that. I answered the phone and confirmed that everything was all set for this afternoon, and then immediately called Aria. It was after noon. Her yoga class would be over, and I could sure use her help.

4
———

"Just line up the bags on the counter top, and then I'll add a catalog and order form to each one," I said.

Aria had been more than willing to come over and give me a hand. My apartment, a two-bedroom loft above an antiques shop, wasn't too far from the studio where she taught. I had about thirty bags lined up along the counter, filled with mini-bottles of hand lotion and bubble bath, and a trial-sized lipstick and nail polish. I really hoped that was enough. I forgot to ask Maggie how many people she was expecting.

"Here, take these from me." I handed Aria a bag of M&Ms I'd been hoarding. "Hide them." At the rate I was popping the chocolate candies into my mouth, I was either going to gain five pounds or end up sick, both of which wouldn't be good.

"Chill out, girlie. It's going to be all good," Aria said.

"I know, I know. I just wish I hadn't forgotten about it. I hate not being prepared. Not that I couldn't use the distraction."

"Are you okay?"

"I guess. It's just so surreal. I know I haven't even begun processing it yet, but what am I going to do? This takes the expression 'wrong place, wrong time' to a whole new level."

"Do you even know what happened?"

"Stabbed. In the heart, no less."

"That's horrific. It would explain the blood." Aria had seen the dried blood on me first-hand yesterday.

"Yeah, and it also makes you think that Roger knew the murderer. At least, well enough to get close to attack like that," I said, recalling what Eric had said.

"You mean he was caught off guard?"

"Yeah, like he didn't expect it, I guess."

"You know, some people are already pointing the finger at Marion."

"Now you sound like Mrs. J. That's just the sort of thing she would say."

"She's not the only one saying it. Honestly, I wouldn't be surprised if it's true."

"Marion? Come on. I don't buy it. Plus, she clearly wasn't the one to put me in a choke hold."

"She might not have done it herself but, with money like hers, she could afford to hire someone. Clearly, you didn't know Roger."

"Like you did?" Aria gave me a look to suggest otherwise. "All right, spill it. What do you know?"

Aria stopped what she was doing and joined me at the table. This had to be good if it required her full attention. "So, get this. Last year, at their neighborhood Christmas party, I was chatting up the neighbors when I ran into Roger and asked if he needed help with anything. They had wait staff and all, but I was just being nice. I don't know what Roger thought I meant, but next thing I knew, he was all touchy feely, flirting with me, refilling my champagne glass and trying to trap me under the mistletoe. At one point, he asked me what my plans were for New Year's Eve. He even offered a private sailing lesson on his boat. Something about his 'big mast' or whatever. I about gagged."

"He did not!"

"I swear he did, and it gets worse. He caught me completely unaware in the hallway when I was putting my coat on ... and kissed me full on the mouth. I was shocked and bolted out of there without telling him off like I should've."

"Where was Marion?"

"She was right there! It was so embarrassing. Everyone saw it, and my non-reaction. They gossiped about it for months. I'm convinced Mrs. J. still thinks I slept with him."

I laughed off Aria's comment, but she was probably right. "How come you never told me about this?"

"It was right after your break up with "He Who Must Not Be Named." I figured you were mad enough at the opposite sex to last a lifetime, without me adding my male drama to the mix."

Aria was right, I was pretty ticked off at the male species after calling off my wedding.

"And I made sure to keep my distance from the pervert ever since. I'm sorry I didn't say anything to you, but I just wanted to forget it ever happened."

I walked over and gave Aria a big hug. "Girl, don't ever keep anything like that from me again. Even if I am neck deep in my own drama." There's no way I would've let Roger get away with assaulting my friend and making her feel less than the awesome person she is. I paused in careful thought. "Do you think Roger normally treated women that way?" I asked Aria.

"I'd bet money on it," she replied.

"Really? I had never gotten that vibe from him."

Roger had always been all-business around me. Maybe he knew I'd kick his ass if he ever tried anything? I'd never know the answer to that, but now I did understand why people were pointing the finger at Marion.

"So, you really think Marion could've done it?" I asked.

"Listen, who knows. All I'm saying is that you won't be seeing her wearing black at his funeral. And I don't blame her. That man was scum."

I thought back to Marion's nutty behavior earlier that day. "I have to admit, she was acting a bit off this morning. I thought she was just trying to keep busy, burn off some nervous energy, but maybe there's more to it," I said.

"Like guilt?"

"Maybe." I really wasn't sure.

"If I were the police, I'd take a good look at her," Aria said.

I thought back to the man who had attacked me. I had no way of knowing if he had been hired or not. It's not like there was a rental van in the driveway.

"Besides, it's always the spouse, isn't it?" Aria added.

She had a point, even if I wasn't ready to admit it.

LADIES FLOODED into South Palm Shore's conference room, like afternoon sunlight through sheer curtains. I couldn't figure out why so many women were there, until I spotted Mrs. J. *God bless that woman.* Her mouth eliminated the need for advertising. I'd like to believe she came because she loved Beauty Secrets' products so much, but I knew better. The whole room was already talking about the murder, and

I could only hope that she wouldn't tell them that I'd been there.

I couldn't worry about that though. Scanning the room, I quickly realized I could easily double my client list tonight, and that had me stoked. That is, if Justine didn't screw it up. Even with her over-sized sunglasses and black bobbed wig on, I spotted her the minute she sat down. I mean, who wears sunglasses inside? *Pathetic drama queen.* That thought circled my mind as I got the demo started.

I kicked things off with a game. One thing clients love more than free samples? Prizes. I was giving away a floppy sunhat in Beauty Secrets' signature violet hue. Mrs. J. eyed the hat the moment she sat down. It matched the hot purple Capri pantsuit she wore perfectly. Mrs. J. was the only woman I knew who could dress head to toe in purple and still look fashionable. Few women possessed such talent. I'd look like a bloated eggplant.

The game was a spinoff of a scavenger hunt; only, the ladies looked for items in their purses. I started it off by asking for easy-to-find items like car keys and gum, before switching to more challenging items like lipstick, earrings, perfume, and photos of grandchildren. Mrs. J. dropped out of the running when I asked for the pair of earrings. She tugged at her ears in a wishful gesture.

The final item on my list was sunscreen. Considering that the prize was a sunhat, and this was a beauty demo, it was a perfect tie in. Luckily, only one of the ladies had all seven items and she turned out to be an older woman named Inez, sitting in the last row. I couldn't see all of her at first, just the top of her sable brown bouffant jumping up and down. For an older lady, she sure had some spunk. She came running down the aisle like a game-show contestant to claim her prize. Imaginary music, complete with bells and whistles, played in my head. Everyone but Mrs. J. clapped and cheered for her. They weren't going to be best friends anytime soon.

Over the crowd, I congratulated Inez for caring so much about her skin. Any woman who carried sunscreen around in her purse knew the importance of protecting her skin and deserved to be rewarded. Inez beamed at the sound of my praise and thanked me repeatedly. She would have given an acceptance speech if I hadn't asked her to retake her seat.

After wrangling in the ladies, the demo continued. Before I knew it, I had talked about every product and given away every free sample I owned. My demo bag was empty except for a couple nail polish remover wipes and a nail file. I'd have to replenish my stash later.

The conference room was quiet as everyone went through the product catalog, page-by-page, writing down their orders. I walked around the room and talked to the ladies individually, promising I'd personally deliver their orders as soon as they came in. Most of them confirmed that they lived at South Palm Shore, which was going to save me a ton of time making house calls. If I could borrow Dad's golf cart for deliveries, it would be even better. Tonight's demo definitely paid off. Justine snuck out before I made it to her row, and I was grateful she didn't talk to anyone on her way out.

Even though the demo was officially over, several of the ladies stayed to chit chat during a coffee-and-cookies reception Maggie had arranged. I debated packing up my products first before hitting the cookie table, but a frosted sugar cookie was calling me from across the room, and I couldn't ignore it any longer. Buttercream frosting held my heart.

I had managed to avoid Mrs. J. so far, but I couldn't help getting sucked into her gossip when I heard her say, "I would've killed him, too, if he'd been my husband, running off with every two-cent tramp, while I suffered through chemo. He got what he deserved."

The ladies nodded in agreement. Inez was the only one who told Mrs. J. she was being distasteful.

"I'm just telling the truth. We all know Roger was about the looks. The minute Marion lost her hair, he was out looking for another one of his Southern sleazes to get his jollies off with. One way or another, he screwed the wrong person. It's the truth, and y'all know it," Mrs. J. said. She paused when she saw I was listening. "We can just thank the Lord that no one else was hurt like our Ziva here. You okay, sug'?" she asked.

I waved off their concern and quickly shifted the focus off me by asking, "What are you ladies all talking about?"

"Oh, you know, Roger's cheating ways and Marion's breast cancer." It was as if Mrs. J. was talking about the weather or what she planned for supper. I tried not to choke on my cookie.

"Didn't she tell you about it?" asked Mrs. J.

"No," I quickly mumbled with my hand over my mouth. I tried to play it cool, but this was huge news to me. I couldn't hide my wide eyes and it didn't take much to get Mrs. J. on a roll.

"Why do you think she was always buying up those beauty products of yours? I'm sure she has just as many wigs, too." I looked at her, dumbfounded. Mrs. J. took that for an answer. "She was trying to keep that man of hers from roaming, but Lord knows it didn't work."

I thought back to all my weekly visits with Marion, and nothing jumped out at me. We'd sip our tea, she'd tell me about the latest charity event she was organizing or what home project she was designing, place her Beauty Secrets order, and that was it. Perhaps I wasn't as intuitive of a beauty representative as I thought. I assumed Marion was like most of my wealthy clients with a love of makeup, and money to spend. I never realized there was something much deeper going on. She certainly never looked like she was battling cancer. Marion was always polished and put together.

"You mean Roger started cheating on Marion after she got sick?" I finally asked.

"Good heavens, no. He started cheating on her years before. It's just when she got sick that he stopped keeping it a secret," Mrs. J. said.

A dozen insults came to mind, but I kept quiet by reminding myself that I was a professional. Trashing clients, even their deserving husbands, was never acceptable. However, that wouldn't stop me from telling Aria she was right about Roger. I wondered if she was right about Marion too. Aria was ready to convict Marion with just the cheating bit. *Wait until I tell her he did it while she was battling breast cancer!*

Mrs. J. read my silence correctly. "I know. Now you see why she'd want to kill him," she said.

Yes, that I did see, but I still had a hard time picturing it. Not that I didn't know what that type of anger felt like. Mr. Ex-fiancé and the cocktail waitress came to mind. But I didn't kill him, I broke up with him—and keyed his car. And yes, the car was expensive, and yes, I kept the ring.

It seemed like I was the only one giving Marion the benefit of the doubt. I wasn't ready to convict her of murder, but she did have my sympathy. Looking around the room, I knew I was the only one. All I had to say was that Marion better pray that, if she ever was formally accused of murdering Roger, her trial was in another town because everyone in that room had already pegged her guilty.

I left the ladies to continue their socializing and went back to packing up my demo, grabbing two cookies along the way, but no matter how sweet the buttercream frosting tasted, it couldn't take the bitterness out of the news I'd just learned.

After the demo, I was too geared up to go home. I had the feeling that I needed an extra-large margarita if I was going to relax tonight, and I knew just the place to go. Rocky's was the best joint around to indulge in liquor and buttery seafood goodness. Dinner at Rocky's would be the perfect remedy to my day. With that thought, I bypassed North Bay Street and headed toward the coast.

This time of year, Rocky's parking lot was fairly empty. Most of the snowbirds had already headed north, and the family vacation rush was still a few weeks away. I parked right up front and walked into the open-aired restaurant. Ceiling fans hummed from the high wooden-beamed ceiling, reminding me of cicadas buzzing on warm August nights. White twinkle lights ran along the bar inside and were cast over the trees outside, like a fishing net full of stars. I took a seat outside under the canopy of lights at one of the checkered tables, and waited for the waitress to come by to light my citronella candle. There was nothing like South Carolina's unofficial mascot, the mosquito, to ruin your evening. I was convinced the bugs were ten times larger and faster down South. Without winter's deep freeze, there was nothing to slow them down. You couldn't swat the suckers fast enough.

I was taking in the scenery and thinking about what I wanted to order when, suddenly, that eerie feeling of being watched washed over me. You know, the one that makes you run up the basement stairs at night or double check to make sure your front door is locked? Yeah, I was having all sorts of creepy feelings in that moment. The bushes rustled to my right, and I thought about getting up to investigate. Cheers and jeers caught my attention from across the bar, instead, and took that thought with them.

"That ball is gone. See ya," hollered the bartender.

"Now that's what I call a home run! Right, Finn?" shouted another man. A couple of loud claps followed in appreciation.

"And you wanted to trade him," replied Finn. For the second time today, I found myself staring. I couldn't believe who it was. Leaning against the bar, watching the game and drinking a Coke, was the shirtless hottie from the marina. Even with his back to me and his shirt on, I was positive it was the same guy. He turned and caught my eye. Yep, it was him all right. So, the hottie had a name ... Finn.

I smiled to say hello. Not wanting to seem too stalker-ish (I swear I didn't follow him here), I broke eye contact and began looking over the menu. Finn must've seen my smile as an invitation because he came over to my table before I finished skimming the appetizers.

"Hey, you look familiar. You work-out by the marina, don't you?" *So, he has noticed me.* This was good.

"Yeah, I think I've seen you down there before too," I replied, thinking, *You're one of the reasons it's my favorite place to work-out.*

"I thought so. I like working out down there too. Usually, I get my run in in the morning before work. I'm Finn, by the way. Finn Jacobs." He outstretched his hand. I was impressed. Most guys nowadays didn't offer a formal introduction.

"Ziva Diaz," I replied and shook his hand. Finn took a

seat across from me, and I tried to play it cool. "So, you work at the marina?" I asked, instead of saying what I really wanted to, which was, *"Mmm, you smell nice."* Motor oil mixed with cologne—rugged, sexual, and sweet all at the same time. I kept my thoughts in check though. After all, I didn't want to freak the poor guy out. In the past, I've been told that I come on a little too intense in new relationships. It was something I was working on.

"That's where you'll find me most days," he replied with a smile.

I believed that. He always seemed to be there no matter what day or time I worked out. Something about the marina made me stop and think for a minute. Then I remembered Aria's disgusting comment from earlier, about Roger's sailboat and his "tall mast," and I had a thought. "Hey, did you by chance know Roger Seibold?" I asked.

"Why, were you a friend of his?" Finn leaned back ever slightly, seeming to judge me against a new set of unknown criteria.

"No, but I know his wife. I'm just trying to help her make sense of a few things," I said, setting the record straight. My tone sounded more defensive than I had intended, but I didn't like the feeling of being judged. "So, did you know him?" I asked.

"Only through the marina. He was usually pulling his boat out of the slip when I was opening up shop."

"Did he normally sail in the morning?" I would've thought Roger would have headed to the office first thing. I was learning that I didn't know much about him.

"Morning, afternoon, evening. The man lived on that boat, practically did *all* his business on it, if you know what I mean." Finn raised his eyebrows.

"So I've heard." Geez, it looked like I was the only one

who didn't know Roger was a sleaze. I couldn't believe Mrs. J. hadn't let something slip before tonight, especially with the way she liked to gossip. I felt so out of the loop.

"So, then you probably know about Ann Marie?" Finn said.

"Who?" That wasn't a name I was familiar with. My heart rate picked up at the thought of gleaning another clue.

"Ann Marie? She was Roger's girlfriend, or whatever you would call her," he said.

"He had a girlfriend? Like, a long-term thing?" This was definite news to me.

Finn nodded yes.

"Like a mistress?" I asked.

"Oh yeah," he replied.

Gross. "No, this is the first I've heard of her. What can you tell me about her? Do you know her pretty well then?"

"Not really. It's just that all overnight guests must be registered through the marina. We started letting it slide after she became a "regular." That, and Roger didn't like all his indiscretions being recorded."

Wouldn't Marion like to get her hands on that book? I wondered if Detective Brandle knew about this. "Has Ann Marie been around the last night or so?"

"I haven't seen her, but it's the weekend."

"So, what does that have to do with anything?" I asked, clearly missing something.

Finn had a boyish grin on his face. "She's, uh, what they call a *performer* at one of the joints outside town."

I laughed. *Nice.* Roger's mistress was a stripper. It seemed fitting. I was betting the only women he could get to sleep with him were the ones he paid. "Not that I've ever seen her strip," Finn clarified, "It's just what my deck hands tell me."

"Oh, sure," I joked with him. "You're Mr. Innocent."

"Swear, Scouts' honor," he replied. Now *that* I could believe. It was easy to picture Finn as a Boy Scout.

Finn changed the subject. "You know, now that I think about it, Roger did have a bit of odd business going on."

"Odd? How so?" I asked.

"Well, it's just that Roger loved his boat so much that I couldn't believe it when I heard he was going to sell it. I just seemed totally out of character."

"Really? Yeah, that is strange. Where did he plan to take these girlfriends of his then? A boat is much classier than a motel room," I said.

"I don't know. Maybe he was going to eventually buy a new one, but it wasn't going to be anytime soon. He wasn't renewing his dock rental either. There's a broker coming to look at the boat tomorrow. I figured the deal would be off with his death, but his wife called and said it was still on."

"Well, at least Marion knew what he was up to this time," I said.

The eerily feeling descended on me again and I looked behind me once more, but this time it was too dark to make out anything. I ignored it and turned my attention back to Finn. He had given me plenty of food for thought. And speaking of food, the waitress was circling the table, trying to decide if she should interrupt us or not, and I was starving. Finn followed my eyes.

"Well, I'd better get going and let you eat."

I didn't want him to leave, but I had to eat something. A few sugar cookies wasn't going to cut it, which is why I said, "Sure, it was nice to finally meet you. Thanks for the info too. Maybe we can go for a run together sometime."

"I'll be hitting the sand tomorrow at six if you're down," he replied.

"As in six o'clock in the morning? Are you flippin' kidding me?" *Did I just say that aloud?*

"What, too early for you?" Finn laughed. "I like to get my run in before it gets too hot."

"I hear you there." Wasn't that the reason I hadn't run this afternoon?

"How about we make it seven then?" Finn offered.

"*That* I can manage," I said.

"Cool. Just come inside Murphy's when you get there." Murphy's was the bait and tackle shop at the marina.

"Okay, sounds good. I'll see you then." I watched Finn walk away, happy that I'd see him the next morning, even if the hour was ungodly. Getting up early two mornings in a row would be rough, but if I could do it for beauty clients, then I definitely could do it for Finn.

The waitress swung back around and I changed my dinner plans, ordering shrimp tacos and a water instead of crab legs and a margarita. Indulging in butter and tequila would only make me sick come sunrise. The mere thought of upchucking anywhere near Finn was beyond mortifying. I would die of embarrassment. Even now, I was regretting that chocolate cake from this morning. *Look at me, changing my eating habits.* Aria would be so proud.

Working out with Finn might turn out to be the best thing for me.

5

*W*hat was I thinking? When my alarm went off at six o'clock I had some serious reservations. Next to Aria, sleep was my best friend, and she almost beat out Finn until the shirtless image of him came to mind before I could drift back to sleep. That one image alone was enough to get me out of bed and put a smile on my face, especially when I considered he might work out that way.

Normally, I'd just brush my teeth and tie up my hair before heading out for a run; but today, I took it a couple steps further by adding lip gloss and mascara to my routine. I had laid out my clothes the night before, going with a pink and black ensemble, which would prevent any wardrobe crisis. I even had my running shoes ready by the front door, with a pair of socks tucked inside. I don't care to admit how many appointments I'd been late to, trying to find a missing shoe.

With no one on the streets and my foot feeling a little heavy, I made it to the marina with ten minutes to spare. Fog rolled in around the docks, and I zipped up my hoodie. It was still a bit chilly by the water. I looked around the docks and couldn't believe how busy they were. I might not have been fully awake, but the fishermen were. Men and women worked about their boats, getting ready to go out for their morning runs, some coming back in.

Finn was exactly where he said he would be—behind the counter at Murphy's. "You made it," he said.

"It's a little early, but I'm here." I couldn't help checking Finn out. He looked good in running apparel, even with his shirt on.

"I just need to drop this paperwork off on Roger's boat, in case we're not back before the broker shows. Chris, I'm taking off," he hollered toward the back. A man with blonde hair tied back in a ponytail, came out to man the front counter. I smiled hello while Finn introduced me.

"We'll be back in a bit," Finn said.

"Take your time. You know we'll slow down here soon," Chris replied.

Finn agreed. I waved goodbye to Chris and then ducked out the front door.

"Are mornings always this busy?" I asked.

"Always. You got the night guys coming in and the morning ones headed out. Boats have to get out there early and get their lines set, or they don't stand a chance," Finn said.

I had no idea fishing was so technical. Guess there was more to it than a hook and a worm. I followed Finn down the docks, eager to take a peek at Roger's infamous boat. Finn led me away from the commercial fisherman and toward the private docks. I doubted any of these boats had fishing poles on them. Heck, I wouldn't even call them boats; they were yachts. This side of the marina was all about luxury. Finn pointed to Roger's sailboat up ahead. It was in a slip on the end, no other boats beside it. The empty space was striking in the otherwise-packed marina. "Roger rented both slips," Finn explained, "It gave him more privacy."

"I see. Who wants witnesses around when you're up to no good?" I said.

"Are you sure you weren't friends with Roger? Sounds like you knew him pretty well." Finn laughed while he spoke. I gave him my best evil eye, but it was only a half-hearted attempt.

Southern Comfort turned out to be the name of Roger's sailboat, and she was a beauty. I was happy to accept Finn's hand when he asked me to come on board. I'd been on plenty of boats before but never a sailboat, and never a vessel as luxurious as this. The ship's dark wood and gold accents were beautiful. I could only imagine how breath-taking she'd look with her sails at full mast, out on the open water. If her owner hadn't been such a creep, I would've accepted an outing in a heartbeat.

"What does something like this go for?" I asked.

"A boat like this? Oh, about half a million," Finn dropped casually.

"As in five hundred thousand dollars? Holy moly. That's a lot of cash." I couldn't imagine dropping that kind of money on a boat, even if I had it to spare. With a price tag that high, I had to see what the cabins below looked like. I started down the steps to take a peek, and stopped short. The smell hit me before I saw her. My eyes found the source a second later. Sprawled out in all her glory on the bed below was who I presumed to be Ann Marie. A pair of black fishnet nylons knotted tightly around her neck. She was dead, no doubt about it. My legs locked and I thought I was going to vomit. The boat swayed beneath me, or maybe I just lost my balance. The stair railing caught me before I fell. I held onto the railing until I found my footing.

Finn started down the steps after me. I held out my arm to stop him. "Ziva, what's wrong?" he asked.

"Go," I said turning around to face him. "Go, go, go!" I pushed him back with each word. Finn stared at me like I'd lost my mind. He stopped at the top of the steps and I scrambled around him, trying to get off that boat and away from it as fast as possible. For all Finn knew, there was a wild animal about to attack us, or a homicidal maniac hiding out below. The second one could've been a real possibility.

"Come on!" I shouted from the dock. Finn looked back at me and then toward the stairs, seeming to make up his mind to go down and investigate for himself.

"Finn!" I screeched as he walked down the steps. I was practically hyperventilating. The dock tilted and the water seemed too close. I sat down and put my head between my legs and tried to pull it together. I could've lived a million lifetimes and done without ever seeing something like that again.

By the time Finn's shaky legs joined me on dry land, I'd already called 9-1-1.

Two days before, I'd never even been at a crime scene, and now I was stumbling upon them left and right. After calling the police, I had gone inside Murphy's to use the bathroom and take a few minutes to calm down. I was gone less than fifteen minutes; but, when I came out, a crowd had already gathered outside. It wasn't hard to locate the action. An orange police barricade blocked the entrance to the docks, and a uniformed officer stood behind it acting as gatekeeper. A female news anchor stood in the parking lot, interviewing an older man wearing a hunter orange fishing vest and tan floppy hat. The man pointed down the dock to Roger's boat where a handful of individuals were gathered. Detective Brandle stood on the dock alongside the boat with Finn, jotting down notes as they talked. I knew, sooner or later, it would be my turn to talk. I chose *sooner*.

No one noticed as I made my way through the crowd. The reporters seemed to be trying to get their facts straight, and the police were busy with crowd control. I walked alongside the weathered cedar walls of Murphy's and kept my eyes on Detective Brandle and Finn. I was hoping one of them would look up so I could get their attention and avoid having to talk to the uniformed officer, who was easily within twenty feet of me. With his arms folded against his chest, and dark sunglasses on, the officer looked like the type of cop you'd have to watch your mouth with or you'd end up in handcuffs before you could blink. Yes, I knew that from experience.

With no support, I walked over to the officer and said in my most professional voice, "Hi, I'm Ziva Diaz. I'm the one who found the body. Can I speak with Detective Brandle?"

The cop eyed me for a long minute. So long, that I felt like saying, "*Did you hear me?*" But I knew where that conversation would land me. Without a word to me, the cop reached for the radio attached to his vest. I couldn't make out what he said exactly, but I managed to hear my name. The whole procedure seemed ridiculous, seeing the detective was standing right behind him, but whatever. I watched down the dock as another uniformed officer approached Detective Brandle and pointed in my direction. Detective Brandle nodded his approval and the guard moved the orange sawhorse aside. I passed by without further ado.

Up close, the detective didn't look any worse for the wear. His white shirt still had the creases in it from the package, but I was coming to expect that. There wasn't much information I could lend, but that didn't stop the detective from asking questions. No, I didn't know Ann Marie. No, I'd never been on Roger's boat before, except for this one time. Finn knew more, but it wasn't enough to blow open the case. Detective Brandle seemed mostly interested in what we were doing there in the first place, but once Finn told the detective about the appointment with the broker and us dropping off paperwork before our morning run, there wasn't much left to explain.

The detective excused himself for a moment and walked away, leaving me and Finn standing alone. Finn fell into a daze and I kept silent. I stared at the sun and tried to gauge what time it was. Today felt like the longest day of my life. Instead of staring at each other, I turned to watch the action on the boat. One of the investigators, a woman wearing a navy-blue jumpsuit and matching baseball cap, kept climbing up and down the stairs leading to the boat's cabin. Each time, she brought up with her a clear plastic bag that she handed off to another investigator. I assumed she was collecting evidence. I started thinking about what I might have touched. I remembered touching the handrail, but that was it. Would the police want my prints? I figured Detective Brandle would let me know if he did.

A camera's flash caught my attention. I looked up, expecting to see the reporter who had taken it, only to realize it was the coroner taking pictures below the deck. My brain made the connection and I turned away, not wanting to risk seeing Ann Marie's body again. It didn't matter which way I looked though. The scene was the same everywhere. A folded metal gurney wheeled its way down the boardwalk toward Roger's sailboat. The wheels clanked rhythmically along the wooden planks, like an old-fashioned rollercoaster climbing its way to the top. Finn and I stepped aside and let the gurney pass. I, for one, didn't want to be standing here when it came back, and neither did Finn. With his hand on my back, he guided me down the dock where we waited for Detective Brandle.

The heat of the sun wasn't helping matters. The morning haze had since burned off, and the sun's temperature was once again set to brutal. I wanted to stick my head inside the ice cooler outside Murphy's to cool off, but decided to lean against it instead. Finn still wasn't up for much conversation, and I didn't blame him. He stood by my side most of the time, only once going inside Murphy's, but he came back a minute later with a couple of cold Cokes. Bless that man. The cold, caffeinated beverage was just what I needed.

After what seemed like forever, Detective Brandle rejoined us. It took longer than any of us would've liked, to finish the interview. Detective Brandle kept getting called away and seemed a bit distracted. Being overworked does that to you. Each time he returned to speak to me, he spent the next ten minutes reading back what we had just said, before asking another question. It wasn't a very efficient system; then again, how could it be when one is being questioned at a crime scene?

When Detective Brandle was, at last, finished with his questions, it was Finn's turn to ask a few of his own. He was mostly curious about the procedure for letting owners onto the boats that shared the main dock with Roger's. Yellow police tape blocked off the side dock to *Southern Comfort*, but the main dock couldn't be blocked off—unless Detective Brandle wanted to deal with a bunch of angry boat owners. There was no question they'd be anxious to survey their boats to make sure nothing was stolen or damaged. After a short deliberation, Detective Brandle decided to keep an officer stationed at the dock's entrance, where he could keep an eye out, at least for the next twenty-four hours. Detective Brandle said that should keep the crime scene junkies at bay, but still allow people to access their property. His plan made sense to me, and Finn agreed.

By the time we were free to go, the crime van was pulling out, taking the remaining reporters with it. The thought of our initial plans to go for a run seemed comical now. I knew it would probably help me unwind, but so would chocolate. I was a bit shocked when Finn even mentioned resuming our running adventure. Turned out, he was a bit more of a hardcore fitness buff than I was. Sure, I didn't like missing a run two days in a row, but I'd get over it. As long as someone pointed me to the nearest piece of fudge, somehow, I'd manage. Finn was disappointed by my explanation, but seemed to understand. Right now, I had murder on my mind and didn't feel like working out or conversing much.

Back home, without any fudge in the house, I went straight for the cookies and drew a bubble bath. Chocolate crumbs floated in the water like a giant glass of milk. I wish I would've grabbed a glass before slipping in, but my mind was too occupied with the case. I tried to break down the facts. At the front of it, two people had been murdered. I didn't think anyone would argue that the murders were related. I'd even wager that the same person murdered them both, but I didn't know that for sure. Maybe Ann Marie murdered Roger and then someone else murdered her. I had to admit, that was a possibility, even if I couldn't understand why.

When it came to suspects, Marion was at the top of my list. I didn't want to believe it, but she had the strongest motivation and seemed to have the most to gain from his death. Although, why Marion wouldn't just divorce Roger was beyond me. And, why kill Ann Marie? It wouldn't be the first time someone was murdered over jealousy, but I just couldn't imagine Marion doing it. There had to be more to the story. I could only hope that once I got Marion's side of the story, I could clear her name from the list; but until then, I had to face the facts. Marion was prime suspect number one.

I tried to think about who else would want to murder both Roger and Ann Marie. Finn had said Ann Marie was a stripper, so maybe there was a link there. Who knows what type of clientele her employer had, or admirers she'd earned? If I wanted to ever get to the bottom of this, I'd have to take a closer look at Ann Marie's professional and personal life.

I wondered how much of this Detective Brandle knew. Neither Finn nor I brought up the stripper part when we were talking to him. Maybe someone else did, but I doubted it. Detective Brandle wasn't quite an ace detective, and he *had* told me to call him with any news. This wasn't news per se, but I could definitely call him and fill him in on my thoughts. I made a mental note to do just that, and sank further into the tub, finally able to relax.

By the time I got out of the tub, I felt almost normal. Well, normal enough to put the murders out of my mind for a few hours and focus on my beauty business. It took a while, but I was able to create accounts for the new clients I'd earned from last night's demo, and input everyone's orders online. Flipping through my binder, I remembered Eric's offer to scan it for me and thought I'd give him a call to set something up. I tried his office number twice but got no answer. Since I was already making calls, I decided to check in with one of my brides, Rachel, to confirm her makeup trial run for this week, and to see if we were still doing a makeover party for her bridesmaids.

Rachel answered on the second ring.

"Hey, Rachel, it's Ziva. Just calling to make sure we're all good for Thursday."

"Ziva? Oh my gosh. I can't believe you're calling. Your friend said you couldn't talk."

At that moment, that was the truth. I was speechless. I had no idea what she was talking about. "Um, what?"

"This girl called and said you broke your jaw. It was wired shut and everything."

"Excuse me?"

"You busted up your face?"

My face was perfectly fine, but I had a feeling Justine's was going to need medical attention when I was done with her. Rachel confirmed it. Not only had Justine told her that I had broken my jaw, but also that I had done it falling down drunk on River Street. Apparently, I had one too many frozen daiquiris and attempted a one-handed cartwheel in a cocktail dress. The pavement caught my face. And here's the thing: back in high school, I was known for my one-handed cartwheels. In fact, I was a cheerleader, and I could tumble circles around Justine. She never made the squad. She clearly wasn't over it.

I smoothed everything over with Rachel and sat fuming for a few minutes, thinking about how I should handle Justine. I usually ignored her, but how was I supposed to ignore this? The woman needed a hobby, or a boyfriend, something to take her mind off me. I'd rarely seen her for the past year, but, out of the blue, she started selling makeup and has been out to get me ever since. The woman needed professional help.

I rolled my eyes so hard I almost fell over. Today sucked.

I had two choices: sit at home and eat more cookies, or get out and do something to keep my mind busy until I figured out how to handle Justine. Something that would make me feel completely wonderful and totally glamourous. Something that I absolutely loved and deserved. Something like ... a pedicure. Yes, a pedicure was exactly what I needed. *Heck, I might even splurge and get a manicure while I'm at it. Pick up a chai latte on the way, too. Ha! Take that, life.*

This last week might've kicked me around a bit, but I wasn't about to lie down.

he next morning, I woke up with energy to spare. My afternoon mani and pedi turned into a full-on spa experience, and it was glorious. My soul thanked me for the time out. But today, I was back at it. I called my attorney and started the paperwork for a defamation suit against Justine. I definitely had her on the hook for slander. I figured it was the more adult way to handle things, versus punching in her face. Next, I tried to reach Detective Brandle, but both numbers sent me to his voicemail. I shouldn't have been surprised, but it was really starting to irk me that he had yet to take or return my calls. I prayed he wasn't the main contact for information regarding the case. If that was true, who knew how many other people's calls were going unanswered. It's not like I had earth-shattering news, but one small detail could've cracked this case, and Detective Brandle would never know if he didn't return my calls.

It seemed the only person, who had her phone on, was Mrs. J. She had called me five times in the past twenty-four hours, asking about her lipstick. I'm no fool. I knew she only wanted to ask me about the murders, which is why I didn't answer her calls. She knew that too. It didn't stop her from calling though. If there was one person you couldn't hide from, it was Mrs. J. I eyed her lipstick on the counter and knew that I couldn't avoid the woman forever. The question was, did I feel up to talking to her *today*?

I was thinking about what I should do, when the news came on. I'm not much of a news person. The reporters always seem to be detailing the latest tragedy or senseless killing. The whole half hour was depressing. The weather forecast was boring too. I was just about to turn off the tube when I heard Roger Siebold's name mentioned, and something about a press release. The reel cut to footage of Eric standing in front of the Siebold's house, releasing a statement. I turned up the volume in time to hear him say, "Roger was a great man, a great member of this community. He will be deeply missed by his family, colleagues, and clients. We know the police are tracking a solid lead, and we are confident that the person responsible will be brought to justice. We ask that if anyone has any additional information, please call the police. Thank you."

I wondered what solid lead the police were tracking, and if there was any way they'd share it with me. Fat chance of that, but maybe Eric had some information he could pass on. That was more likely. The reel cut back to the newsroom where the anchor provided additional information on the case, including the "breaking news" they'd just learned about a woman who was assaulted at the Siebold home earlier in the week. The police had yet to release the details of the attack, including the woman's identity, but the anchor hoped to have further details for the five o'clock news.

I felt sick. I hadn't even considered the media. That's all I needed—reporters knocking on my door, and the murderer knowing where I lived. *Mrs. J. had better keep her mouth shut.*

There was no doubt in my mind that she watched the news every day. If there was a tip line, I was sure she'd be calling in to give out my information. Heck, she'd probably offer to drive them over to my place if it meant she could get on television. That sealed it. I needed to pay Mrs. J. a visit today, so I could stay on her good side and get her to keep quiet about all this.

The next story cut to Detective Brandle, giving a statement about the recent break-ins. Three businesses had now been hit, with Cognac's Cigar & Whiskey Bar being the latest. It wasn't a formal statement, but the type you get when reporters hammer a person for details. The detective looked composed but exhausted, like he wanted to be anywhere else but there, answering the reporters' questions. His face was starting to resemble a basset hound with his droopy eyes and saggy cheeks. *Someone get that man some regenerating cream and a glass of water.* Who knew how many free radicals he had floating around in his system with a face that dehydrated. I figured he must have been sustaining himself on coffee and cop fare. Definitely not healthy. I had no room to talk, but at least I worked out. Okay, I worked out sometimes. The detective didn't have time for that. How he was assigned to more than one major case was beyond me. During the questions, Detective Brandle stated that they were following up with leads, and that if anyone had seen anything unusual, or if they saw anyone acting suspicious downtown, to call the police. Detective Brandle left it at that and excused himself to head inside the station.

I pondered the information I'd just received from the news report. All the targeted businesses had one thing in common: they all catered to high-end clientele. No surprise there. After all, a true crook would hit up some place with valuable contents.

I sympathized with Detective Brandle's workload but found myself wishing he'd devote more time to the Siebold case; or better yet, assign someone else to it. I tried the detective's phone again. This time, it went straight to voicemail. That sealed it. First stop was Mrs. J.'s and then I was off to talk with Eric. It was time for some answers.

THE CLOCK READ a few minutes before one by the time I headed to Mrs. J.'s. She called two more times before I could make it out the front door. You'd think I knew who killed Kennedy the way she was on me for information. I knew I was in trouble when I pulled into her driveway and saw her sitting on the front porch, without a sweet treat waiting for me. *Darn it. I was hungry too.*

"Afternoon, Mrs. J.," I said.

"Afternoon yourself, girl. Do you know how many beauty consultants are in my neighborhood? I could give all my business to someone else if you're too busy to keep up with your clients."

I knew exactly who Mrs. J. was referring to. No way was I letting Justine steal Mrs. J. from me. Not that I thought she'd really leave me, but I wasn't about to chance it.

"Sorry, Mrs. J. You don't have to wait another minute. Here you go." I handed the gift bag over. Mrs. J. left it on the table without even opening it. *That's what I thought.* She didn't care one ounce about the lipstick. "Well, if that's all you need, I should probably get going. I don't want to keep any of my other clients waiting," I said.

"Well now, wait a second, sug'. I doubt your clients would mind one bit if you took a minute to catch up with old Mrs. J."

"I don't know." I eyed my truck, ready to hop in it and take off.

"Just have a seat for a second. You wouldn't believe what Patsy Ann told me this morning." I had a feeling I knew exactly what the deputy's wife had said. I sat and waited for Mrs. J. to continue.

"So, is it true? Did you really find another dead body?" she asked. I thought about the best way to explain what had happened, but came up short. "Good heavens, that's what I thought. Patsy Ann said you must be a mess by now, but I told her if anyone could trip over a couple dead bodies and come up smiling, it was you."

Technically, I didn't trip over either dead body, but I knew what Mrs. J. was getting at. "Thanks, Mrs. J.," I said.

"I'm not sure if you're really lucky, or unlucky, sweet girl," she said.

"Honestly, I'm not sure either. Hey listen, I know reporters would love to catch wind of my name, but can you do me a favor and keep what you know on the DL? The last thing I need is a bunch of reporters hounding me."

"Of course. I wouldn't dream of saying anything." Mrs. J. acted as if the thought otherwise never crossed her mind, but I knew better.

"I'm serious. I want to lie low, at least until the case is solved. I don't need the murderer knowing my name or where I live."

Mrs. J. looked at me for a long moment. The seriousness of this seemed to be sinking in. This wasn't the usual town gossip I was asking her to withhold. "You have my word," she said. For whatever reason, I knew she meant that.

"Enough with all this murder business. I know what you need. Here, come inside. I've got a fresh batch of peach cobbler cooling on the counter. There's plenty to share," Mrs. J. said.

I followed Mrs. J. inside and sat at the kitchen table, and let her fuss over me.

"How's Marion holding up?" she asked with her head in the freezer.

The picture of Marion power walking around her front yard came to mind. I wondered what Mrs. J. would make of it. She'd probably consider it as good as a confession in her book. I kept that memory to myself. "She seems okay, keeping busy," I said, which was the truth. "I haven't talked to her in the last day though."

Mrs. J. joined me at the table, with two bowls of warm peach cobbler topped with vanilla ice cream.

"Milk?" she asked. I couldn't answer. Warm, sweet glaze and crumbly, cinnamon topping, blended with the cool ice cream to create heaven in my mouth.

"It's good, isn't it, sug'?" Mrs. J. went back to the fridge and poured me a glass of milk.

"You are too good to me." I licked the back of the fork.

"Hush now, honey. You deserve it. Besides, sometimes you need a lil' something sweet to erase the sour," she said. I couldn't argue with that.

Mrs. J. joined me back at the table. "Poor Marion. You know, that husband of hers was no good. She doesn't deserve any of this."

I couldn't have agreed more. "What do you think happened?" I asked.

"I tell you what, I'm not one hundred percent sure, but there's more going on. *That,* I know." Mrs. J. leaned forward over her bowl of cobbler and whispered, "You see, just last week, I caught Marion sneaking out of Dr. Michelson's at the crack of dawn."

"Wait, what?!" I shook my head, trying to keep up. Where did that come from?

"Mmm-hmm. You know Dr. Michelson," Mrs. J. said.

"Yeah, everyone knows Dr. Michelson. He's like the Mister Rogers of Port Haven." Seriously, the man exuded honesty and compassion. He wasn't about to go off gallivanting with a married woman. I wasn't buying it. He just wasn't scandalous like that.

"Well, let me tell you, Marion and your Mister Rogers have had the hots for each other for years. Years!" she insisted.

"What? No way," I said.

"You better believe it," she replied.

"Mrs. J., seriously? How do you know something scandalous was even going on?"

"Oh, honey, if you would've been there, you would've known it too," she said.

I eyed her, waiting for the story that I knew was about to follow.

"Okay, so you know how Dr. Michelson's office is next door to Sweet Thangs?" Mrs. J. asked.

That was a rhetorical question. Come on. Me? Candy? Cookies? Anyone who knew me knew I loved Sweet Thangs. It was my favorite spot to indulge in a sugar rush.

"Well, last week, I stopped by bright and early to drop off a fresh batch of my pralines. Lately, I can't seem to make them fast enough. Last time, they sold out in two days. Lordy, can you imagine? Couldn't disappoint the customers, now, could I? Anyhow, so there I was, waiting for them to open, and that's when I saw them."

"Who?" I asked, covering my mouth while I talked.

"Marion and Dr. Michelson! I could see right up into his window. Oh, honey girl, you should've seen them. His hand was brushing her cheek, and I know that look. They either just got done doing something, or were about to start."

"Seriously?" I grew silent, unsure of what to think. "There could still be a totally plausible explanation," I said after a minute, even though, at that moment, I couldn't think of one.

"Sure, I'll let you think about that one for a while," Mrs. J. said with a smirk.

"Okay, so let's say Marion was hooking up with Dr. Michelson. So what? Are you saying Dr. Michelson killed Roger?"

"Oh, good heavens, no," she said.

Well, that was at least one thing we could agree on.

"He might be after a little hanky panky, but he's not about to kill someone over it," Mrs. J. said.

Oh my. "Mrs. J.!"

"Well, I'm just saying…," Mrs. J. trailed off before adding, "Listen, I actually don't know what's going on with Marion, Dr. Michelson, this, that, or whatever other girlfriend of Roger's. But, what I do know is, if there's one person who would've really liked to see Roger Siebold dead, it would be his son."

Mrs. J. was just full of bombshells this afternoon.

"Wait, what son?" I asked. I had lived in Port Haven my whole life and never knew Marion and Roger had a son. I was positive Marion never mentioned having children. I had just assumed she and Roger married later in life, and kids hadn't been an option.

"Doesn't surprise me you don't know him. Philip's a bit older than you. And it's been what, fifteen years I'm guessing, since he's stepped on this side of the Mason-Dixon," replied Mrs. J.

"Really? How come?" I asked.

"Well, I don't like to gossip," Mrs. J. said.

Since when? I thought.

"But rumor has it, it had something to do with Roger's business. Heard his daddy cut him right out of it. I don't know the details, but whatever happened sent Philip straight to New York, and I don't think he's been back since. Not like the two ever got along to begin with, mind you. Marion was always in the middle, trying to make peace, but Lord knows it never worked."

"That's sad," I said. "It must've been something really nasty to keep him away for that long." I couldn't think of anything that would keep me away from my parents for fifteen years, especially from my dad. I was a daddy's girl through and through.

"Let me tell you, Roger was rotten to that boy his whole life. Don't know what he had against him. He seemed like a sweet kid to me, but I guess the business mess was the final blow."

"Yeah, I guess," I said.

"You know, people can only handle so much, and I'm guessing Philip just had enough."

Mrs. J. gave me plenty to think about, and I now had even more information to share with Detective Brandle. That was, if he ever called me back. Mrs. J. might be convinced of Philip's guilt; but to me, he was just another suspect to add to the list, along with Dr. Michelson ... if I could believe it.

On that note, I wrapped up my beauty business with Mrs. J., thanked her for the peach cobbler, and headed out to track down my next source. I was really hoping Eric was at his office. If not, I had no idea how to get a hold of him.

7

"*S*IS," a woman said in a tart voice.

"Hi, is Eric Pérez available?" I asked.

"No, he's not," the woman replied.

I hung on the line waiting for further explanation, but that was all I got. Nice, huh?

"Okay, can I leave him a message then?" I asked.

"You can, but I don't know when he'll get it," she replied.

Silence again. Was this woman the receptionist or not?

"Does he have voicemail?" I asked.

"No."

Of course, not.

"Okay ... I don't suppose you could give me his cell number?" Even I could hear the hopeful tone in my voice. I knew it was a long shot, but the woman actually snorted at me. *What a witch.* It took every ounce of patience for me not to snap at her.

"Never mind then. I'll reach him later," I huffed.

"You do that," she replied and hung up, just like that.

I was beyond ticked and was thinking I had liked it better when no one had answered the phone. I had no idea what that woman's problem was, but I wasn't in the mood to be messed with. I wanted to talk to Eric and see what he had to say, and that woman was the only one standing in my way. I wondered if she would be as rude in person? There was only one way to find out. Besides, she didn't say he wasn't in, just that he wasn't available. Maybe I'd get lucky and catch him in the office.

Just over an hour later, my car approached the South Carolina/Georgia border. I didn't need to read the state marker or see the Talmadge Bridge in the distance to know the city was close. The sight of five gentlemen's clubs in a quarter-mile-span, was evidence enough. By day, the pink stucco buildings with their gravel-dirt parking lots and dusty windows, looked like something straight out of a horror flick; but by night, the same parking lots were filled with flashy sports cars and custom motorcycles. The blinking lights drew the men in like mosquitoes to a bug zapper. Of course, I was instantly reminded of Ann Marie and wondered which club she had worked at. *Since I'm here, I should stop and ask around, maybe come back at night when the girls come in. Heck, I could even drop off a few catalogs.* Now there was a way to perk up business. I bet they went through a ton of makeup. Of course, I'd wear rubber gloves when collecting payment. That thought gave new meaning to the phrase "dirty money."

I had never been to Siebold Investment Securities before, but downtown Savannah's city squares weren't hard to navigate. After all, they were the heart of the city, and I had the address. The flow of traffic led me straight into the city. Swamp oaks, cement Civil War statues with brass nameplates, gothic architecture, and trolley tours fought for my attention. An eclectic group of people called downtown Savannah, home. For every attraction, there was a person who was just as fascinating. They'd tell you their story if you asked, or if you stood still long enough. I knew that first-hand from one late night I had spent in the city. Somehow, I had ended up talking politics with a homeless man for half an hour. I have no idea how the conversation even started. And it wouldn't be Savannah without the voodoo, ghost stories, and cemeteries. They were tourist attractions in their own right.

A gold-plated address told me I was in the 700th block. *Roger and Eric's office should be two blocks ahead.* I followed the squares up and scanned the buildings. To my left, the initials SIS caught my attention. The ten-inch tall, black letters with gold outline were etched onto the front window of a two-story, red brick building across the street. *That has to be it.* A metered spot was opening in front of me. Perfect timing. I waited for the vintage VW Bug to back out, and I attempted to parallel park the pickup. Good thing I had skills, because the spot was tight.

Thirty minutes were left on the meter, enough time to hopefully talk to Eric and come back without getting a ticket. I cut across the center square and admired the surrounding atmosphere. Like the rest of downtown Savannah, the outside of SIS was accented with a low, wrought-iron gate that had been overgrown with honeysuckles. Parts of the neighborhood were residential. Boutiques, businesses, condos, and houses blended together. Gas-lit sconces, gated front gardens, wrought-iron arbors, and white ceramic birdbaths equally accented the architecture.

It appeared that the investment firm only rented out the lower left side of the building. The other side housed a cigar shop, with a hat boutique upstairs. From the top window, it looked like headquarters for Mardi Gras. Bursts of red-and-silver sequined hats with purple-and-gold feathered accents glimmered in the sunlight, reminding me of Aria's and my trip to New Orleans a few years back. Downstairs, the cigar shop's perched-open door let the sweet smell of tobacco roll out and mix with the scent of honeysuckles outside. Now that was a scent they should bottle.

I resisted the urge to go inside the boutique, and reached for the opposite door. Like the window, the initials SIS had been etched onto the door's beveled glass. Below the initials, in the same gold lettering, were the words *Solid Investment Securities*. I had to look twice to make sure I read it right. Roger must have changed the word *Siebold* to *Solid* after Eric came on board. I made a mental note and cataloged the scent in case I ever developed my own beauty line.

A brass bell fastened to a leather strap clanked twice against the top of the door when I walked in. The receptionist looked just as tart in person, with her designer summer suit, black-rimmed glasses, and blunt blond bob. She glanced up at my appearance and dismissed me just as quickly. This woman needed an attitude adjustment.

Eric's voice came from the door to my left, and I was thrilled that he was in. My hunch had paid off. I turned and found him in his office, looking as charming as ever. He was standing over an impressive desk with the phone in one hand and the receiver in the other, looking as if he'd stepped off the pages of a men's fashion magazine. His suit was dark and his shoes were shiny. I had no idea where he'd learned to dress, but I was impressed.

"Yes?" Tart asked me.

"Me? Oh no, I see who I need. Thanks," I said.

"Mr. Perez is busy today and is not meeting with clients," she snapped.

"Well, good thing I'm not a client then." *Ooh, burn*, I thought. I peeked my head back toward Eric's office and caught his eye. He smiled and held up his finger, signaling he'd just be another minute.

I don't think he even made me wait a minute. It seemed like two seconds later, he was striding across the room to greet me. "Ziva, good to see you," he said, giving me a quick kiss on the cheek.

"Sorry for just dropping by," I replied.

"Don't apologize, you're always welcome. Step into my office," he said.

I resisted the urge to say "*Ha!*" to Tart and, instead, accepted Eric's invitation. I followed him without a backward glance.

Like the lobby, Eric's office was full of dark-wooded and leather furniture. It appeared to have the original planked hardwood floors too; although, it was hard to tell, as most of the floor was covered by a large burgundy and gold oriental rug. The cognac set and a globe stand in the corner completed the room. Except for a small pile of papers on his desk, the office was clean and clutter free.

"So, what can I do for you?" he asked.

"Well, I saw you on the news this morning and heard you mention something about the police tracking a lead? I was just wondering what you could tell me."

"I did say that, didn't I?" He twisted his lips to the side in thought for a moment.

"Oh man, you mean it's not true?" I asked. *Crud*. Maybe my trip had been a waste of time after all.

"Honestly, I don't know. They could be tracking a lead, but they haven't said anything to me. I just threw that part in because I thought it sounded good, you know? Thought it might make the killer nervous."

I tried to hide my disappointment. "Yeah, that's probably not a bad idea. So, no word yet?"

"Not yet. I've called Detective Brandle a couple times, but he hasn't called me back yet."

"Yeah, me either." My faith in the detective slipped another notch.

"Did you bring your binder with you?" Eric asked.

"Ugh, no. I totally forgot. I was going to, but got side-tracked," I said.

"Bring it by next time," he said.

"Sure, and give me a call if you hear anything, okay?" I fished one of my cards out of my purse and handed it over.

"Of course," Eric replied.

I felt defeated and really thought that meeting with Eric would've eased my mind or provided me some other clue, but it did neither.

"Thanks. Well, I know you're busy. I'll let you get back to work." I turned to walk out.

"You don't have to rush out. Why don't you join me for lunch?" As soon as Eric asked, his phone rang.

"I'm sorry, I can't. It sounds like you're pretty busy, too," I said.

Eric ignored the phone and gave me his full attention. We stared at each other for a second, and heat rushed through my veins. He was intense.

"Next time then," he said.

"Next time." I waved goodbye and walked out.

Eric's eyes followed me as I left, and I tried not to smile. It was hard not to, with a man that good looking checking me out. It had been a while since I'd let any man in my life. Maybe it was time to rethink that.

I LEFT SIS and headed to the marina. Technically, I had

work to do, like restock my beauty bag and clean out all last campaign's catalogs; but first, I wanted to get caught up with Finn. I figured since we'd found Ann Marie's body together, he was just as vested in this mess as I was.

The marina parking lot seemed unusually full for a Tuesday afternoon. I parked in the back corner of the lot and walked in, looking for any sign of Finn. A gunmetal gray pickup truck was parked in the sun-scorched crusty grass alongside Murphy's. I knew it had to be his.

For all the cars parked out front, the marina itself was surprisingly empty. *Well, I guess that shouldn't be a surprise.* People didn't usually come to the marina to sit on their boats, especially on a gorgeous day like today.

An old man with white hair and round-rimmed glasses perched on the end of his nose, smiled at me from behind his newspaper when I walked inside Murphy's. He looked like Geppetto from *Pinocchio.* I had to smile back.

The old man folded the newspaper down on the counter and said, "Well, hello, Miss. What can I do for you?" I supposed something about my appearance told him I wasn't there to buy bait or tackle.

"Hi, I was looking for Finn. Is he around?" I scanned the store, but didn't see him.

"So, you're the pretty little thing that's been on his mind lately," the old man replied.

"Oh, I don't know about that." I smiled and left it at that. Trust me, it was hard. I really wanted to ask more about Finn's mind and what more "Geppetto" knew.

"I'm Mr. Murphy," said the man.

"Oh, so this must be your place." I extended my arms to sweep the entire area.

"That's right. Murphy's been mine since 1969. Before

that, it was my dad's." Mr. Murphy stared out the window. "And someday, it'll be Finn's."

"Oh, you're Finn's dad?" I asked.

"Something like that," Mr. Murphy replied. "He's just docking up right now." Mr. Murphy motioned behind him.

I looked out the window over his shoulder and saw Finn tying off one of the charter boats. Just like the first time I saw him, he was shirtless and sporting a red bandana—a sight a woman could get used to. *Damn.* He didn't have the style that Eric possessed, but he didn't need it. I checked my libido before it got me into trouble, and walked to the cooler in the back of the store to get two Cokes. Mr. Murphy waved me off when I attempted to pay. "Looks like you know my boy. Don't worry about those," he said.

"Are you sure?" I asked.

"Go on. It looks like he might need your help," he replied.

I seriously doubted that, but I thanked him anyway and walked out.

Finn was gathering up his gear on the boat when I reached him. Four men passed by me on the dock, already telling fish stories. You know, the type where the fish grows by the inch, and the fight lasts an hour longer with each telling. Never mind that they had all been there to witness it. The battle would be deemed epic by the time they got home.

Finn glanced up at me walking down the dock, and did a double take. I waved with one of the Coke bottles in my hand and smiled, pleased, despite my best efforts to see the expression on *his* face.

"Hey, Ziva, come on board," he said when I reached him. Finn came over to the side of the vessel and offered me his hand for balance. I handed him one of the Cokes first and then took his hand and attempted to step on board. I was grateful for the assistance. There was less than a foot gap between the dock and the boat, but I was paranoid that I would slip and fall in. Luckily, that didn't happen.

As soon as I had my sea legs, Finn let go of my hand and went about clearing off a space for me to sit. Fishing rods stuck out of the boat's side holsters, and two huge duffle bag-like tackle boxes cluttered the aisle way. To my left, the port-side rail had layered fish gills and blood stuck to it, making a macabre papier-mâché paste. It was disgusting and very un-girly. Fishing looked like a dirty business, and not one I was looking to get into. Beauty demos were way more glamorous.

Finn removed a stack of bright blue US Coast Guard-approved floating cushions off one of the captain's chairs. I searched the seat for any hooks or other nasty fishing things before taking a seat.

Finn sat atop the back of the chair opposite from me, and threw his white shirt over his shoulder. I may have sighed.

"So, what's up?" he asked.

"Not much. I was just out and about. Thought I'd stop by and see what you were up to." I lied, and it wasn't even a very good one.

Finn eyed me for a minute, not believing a word I'd just said. "Really, is that all?" He twisted open the top of his soda and pressurized fizz hissed out. He took a drink and waited for me to say more.

"Okay, you know that's not why I'm here. I guess you could say I've been obsessing over all this and thought I'd come down and catch you up to speed. Well, and get your take."

Finn realized I was being serious. He glanced around the

docks and then back over his shoulder. "I'm almost done here. Chris can finish up. You want to grab something to eat?" I honestly wasn't hungry, but I didn't want to turn down two lunch offers in one day.

Finn saw the look on my face. "How 'bout a drink then?"

Now *that* was something I could agree to.

---

8

*F*inn offered to drive, and I hopped into the truck that I'd pegged as his earlier. His truck made my little pickup look silly. It was a "man's truck" with extra-large tires, a top-notch sound system, and all-leather interior.

Neither one of us said much as he drove down Highway 17. I wasn't even sure where we were going; but if they served alcohol, I didn't really care. A few minutes of silence was all it took for me to start thinking about the case.

"So, what's on your mind?" Finn asked, picking up on my train of thought.

"Well, this morning I stopped by my client's house, Mrs. J., and she was talking about Marion. Did you know they have a son?" I asked.

"Who does?"

"Exactly." I kicked off my sandals and tucked my legs underneath me while continuing to talk. "So, Marion and Roger have this son, Philip, only Mrs. J. said the guys had a falling out awhile back, and they hadn't been on good terms since. Actually, the two never got along."

"Wonder what the story is there?" Finn said.

"Yeah, I wonder too. Mrs. J. actually didn't know the details."

"Did you tell Detective Brandle about this?"

"Haven't had a chance, but there's more. Mrs. J.'s convinced Marion and Dr. Michelson are also having an affair."

"Dr. Michelson? Wait, the family doctor? Really?"

"Apparently. I mean, I wouldn't blame her with having a husband like Roger, but not with Dr. Michelson. None of it makes sense. I keep coming back to it; but, if they were both so unhappy, why not just get a divorce? That's the story I really want to know."

"Yeah, I hear ya. So, what's your take on this Dr. Michelson? Do you think he did it?"

"I hope not. The man's been my doctor since I was a kid. I couldn't picture anyone less likely to murder someone. Marion either, for that fact. They just don't seem the type."

"There's a murder type?"

"You know what I mean."

"Love's a powerful motivator. People do all sorts of crazy things in the name of love." Finn smiled.

"True, but it still seems pretty far-fetched. I'd really like to meet Philip, though, and get a feel for him." I had already made up my mind to meet the guy, I just had to figure out when and where.

"Wait, wait, wait. Promise me you're not going to go off and meet up with him on your own. Please?" Finn pleaded.

"Don't worry. I'm not planning on it. I'm just saying I'd like to meet him." I smiled a little at his concern for me.

Finn pulled off the highway and turned into a graveled parking lot. Bits of stone crunched under the tires, and a brown dust cloud rolled over the hood. Finn swung the truck around and parked beside the only two other vehicles in the lot. I surveyed the white, cylinder-shaped brick building in front of us for a sign, but all I saw was a faded beer banner advertising two-dollar drafts. That was good enough for me.

Finn led the way to the windowless door, and I let him go in first. My eyes took a second to adjust to the dim light. It was like walking down into a basement—dark, cool, and damp. A row of dusty rectangular windows lined the wall below the ceiling, letting in enough sunlight for me to see the dust particles floating in the air.

Laughter drew my attention over to the bar, where two old men were talking up the young bartender like I'm sure they did every day. She didn't seem to mind though. The megawatt smile she wore never left her face. From the looks of it, she was used to dirty old men.

We walked over to a four top. Finn pulled back a battered vinyl barstool and offered me a seat. "You want a beer?" he asked.

"That'd be great," I replied while sitting.

"Hey, Kat, two drafts, and make 'em tall," Finn hollered over his shoulder.

"Sure thing, Finnie. You want me to turn the game on?" she asked.

"No, that's okay. Thanks though," Finn replied.

"Let me know if you change your mind," she replied.

Finnie? If you asked me, the bartender looked a little young for Finn to be hooking up with, but I wasn't going to say anything.

I scanned the photos on the brown wood-paneled walls. There wasn't anyone famous, just collages of local faces celebrating good times. Nothing about the bar's beer signs and scratched hardwood floors were fancy. The place didn't have a dance floor, Keno, or music. From the smell of it, there was only bar food and alcohol. Really, what else did one need?

Kat dropped off our beers, along with a can of Coke. "For the road," she said when Finn looked up. The jealous vibe rolling off Kat was strong. Maybe Finn should've thought twice before bringing another girl into Kat's territory. I ignored the comment and looked down at the plastic menu that also served as the placemat, until she walked away.

"You know how much sugar's in that can?" I tried to hide the annoyance in my voice, but I was really uncomfortable in that moment.

"We all have our vices," Finn said with a smile, but pushed the can aside. It was stupid, but the simple action made me feel better. Finn laughed.

"What's so funny?" I asked.

"You," he replied. "Kat's my kid sister."

Oh. Was I really that transparent? I laughed at myself. "Well, that was very nice of her then. I'd hate to be stepping on another girl's toes," I said.

"Don't worry, there's no one else's toes to be stepping on," he said with an intense smile.

Oh great, now we were talking in code about Finn's relationship status. *Gah.* I had to admit, though, it was nice to know he was single.

The smell of the fryer heating up made my stomach gurgle, and my thoughts shifted. I was glad we had stopped somewhere that served food. Next to the ads for pest control and plumbing, was a myriad of choices—everything fried— from okra and pickles, to battered mushrooms and jalapeno poppers. I skipped the small stuff and copied Finn, going with the fish and chips when Kat came back for our order.

We both took long swigs of our beers and contemplated

the case. My mind filed through the list of suspects, each one as improbable as the next.

"What about the mistress? asked Finn, picking up our earlier conversation.

"Ann Marie? What about her?" I asked.

"Do you think she's the reason they're both dead?"

"Yeah, I thought about it. It's worth looking into, don't you think?"

"I agree," replied Finn.

"You want to go with me to check out the clubs?" I asked. I was hoping a former patron or coworker could provide a detail or two we were missing, add another piece to the puzzle, or a suspect worth checking out.

"When were you thinking of going? Tonight?" he asked.

"I wasn't planning on it but sure, why not? The sooner the better," I said.

"How about nine o'clock? We can meet up at the marina," he offered.

"Yeah, that works for me." And it would give me plenty of time to figure out what questions to ask and, more importantly, what to wear.

Talk about a tricky wardrobe situation. Dress too provocatively, and you're sure to garner the wrong kind of attention; dress too conservatively, and you look like you're judging. The key was balance, and I found it with a cute pair of jean shorts, strappy sandals, and an off-the-shoulder black shirt. The look said *I have style* not *I give lap dances*. Finn was waiting outside Murphy's when I pulled up, and I motioned for him to get in.

"Any idea what club she worked at?" I asked as he got situated.

"I asked around and the guys said The Palms," he replied.

"That's the one with all the neon, right?" Finn thought about it. "Oh, don't act like you don't know," I teased.

"Honestly, I don't for sure, but I think that's the one." Finn's quick insistence on his innocence was kind of cute. He had a likable personality.

Finn and I spent the forty-five-minute drive trying to figure out what our plan of action was, which we still hadn't figured out when we arrived. The gentlemen's clubs were packed. Billboards flashed words like *Amateur Night* and *$3 Jager Bombs* in blue and green LED lights while the words *Stopless Topless* scrolled in a marquee above one club's door.

The Palm's parking lot was just about full, and it wasn't even quite ten o'clock yet. Finn paid the ten-dollar cover charge for both of us, and the doorman unclasped the red rope for us to enter. If a strip club could be considered classy, this would be it. You would've never guessed it from the outside. Gold and glass seemed to be the theme, from the stage accents to the crystal chandeliers and mirrored walls. Two girls were preforming on stage, using the same pole, and let me tell you, that took talent. Finn and I chose to sit in one of the half-moon booths that hugged the walls, while deciding our next move.

A waitress named Kitti, with an *i*, she informed us, came over to take our drink order. Of course, Finn went with a Coke and I joined him. I learned that if the girls take it all off, the club couldn't serve alcohol. That was too bad because I could sure use a real drink and would've had a pre-drink before heading out tonight, if I hadn't planned on driving.

Kitti's personality was as bright as the gold tassels covering her chi-chis, and I took it as an opening. I was hoping she'd be as outgoing as her outfit or, rather, lack thereof. "Hey, Kitti. My name's Ziva, and this is Finn. Listen, I was wondering if you could help us out. I'm trying to find anyone who knew my friend Ann Marie," I said.

Kitti opened right up. "We all knew Ann Marie. I just can't believe she's gone. She was a hell of a performer. Let me tell you, the men just loved her, and she loved them."

"Yeah, that's what I heard, and what I want to talk to you about," I said.

"What do you want to know?" she asked.

"Well, the police are clueless as to who killed her. I just can't sit back and do nothing. I was wondering if you had any ideas? Like maybe she had an ex-boyfriend with a grudge, or a patron who went a little too far with his admiration?"

"Nah, nothing like that. She was loved by everyone, especially Roger. Man, he was so in love with her. Bought her all that jewelry. Took her on those fancy trips. I was so jealous," Kitti said.

"Anyone else jealous?" I asked.

"No, not like that. She had it all, that's all. And now, it's just so sad." I noticed a good-looking man, dressed to the nines, eyeing us the same moment she did. "Listen, I gotta get back to work. I'll be back in a minute with those Cokes," she said.

The man summoned her, and I assumed he was her boss. Maybe it was the suit or the gelled-back hair, but something about him reminded me of the mafia. I got the impression that he'd have his eye on us for the remainder of the evening.

Word got around that we were friends of Ann Marie's,

and a couple more of the girls stopped by. The story was always the same: the trips, the jewelry, how in love she and Roger were. The fact that he was married was irrelevant.

"They were perfect together," said one of the girls from the pole-dancing duo from earlier. "Like, they had what it took to make it," she continued.

Finn sat back and let me do the talking. "Did you know he was married?" I asked.

The girl shrugged her shoulders as if to say *so what*. "Maybe you should talk to his wife then. I'd be pissed if my husband was in love with another woman. And trust me, they were in love," she said.

"You could say that," chimed in a girl named Tara, with peacock feathers covering her lady bits.

"If Roger gave her everything, then why did Ann Marie still perform?" I asked.

"Because Roger loved to see her up there. Made him feel all alpha. And she made bank. No one brought in more cash than Ann Marie," said Tara. That made sense. If you were good at your job and liked it, why quit? From the sound of it, no one could deny that Ann Marie was talented. No one could also say who'd want to kill her. "Listen, we'd all love to say and chat, but Boss Man doesn't pay us to socialize. We'd better get back to it."

"Unless you want a dance?" Tara asked.

"No, I'm good," Finn replied.

"I wasn't talking to you," she replied.

Oh jeez. "No thanks," I replied. "I got all the action I need right here." I put my arm around Finn's waist and he played along.

"Okay, well, let us know if you change your mind. You can join in too if you'd like," Tara said to Finn.

"Thanks, I'll keep that in mind," he said.

The girls got back to work, and I removed my arm from Finn's waist.

"Well, that was interesting," he said. I wasn't sure which part he meant, but I agreed with him.

It was about midnight by the time we were ready to leave. I left my business cards with a couple of the girls, which, of course, led to us talking shop. I may have even managed to score a new client or two. All in all, I'd say it was a productive evening. I would've tried to chat up the boss man before leaving, but didn't see him on our way out.

The buzz of the club had felt good. It was beautiful night. I was out with a cute guy, and I didn't have anywhere to be in the morning. For a few minutes, I had even managed to forget about Roger and Ann Marie entirely; that is, until we got into the car. The silence was unnerving. Talk about doing a one-eighty. Mrs. J. once said that denial was more than a river in Africa, and now I knew what she meant. I couldn't deny this past week's events—the murders, being assaulted, finding Ann Marie's dead body. It was almost too much. Paranoia is best kept at bay. As soon as you acknowledge it, fear takes over. I was headed for a tailspin.

Finn caught on in a second. "You all right?" he asked.

"Yeah." With the way my voice sounded, even *I* didn't believe me. I stared out the windshield across the parking lot, acutely aware of every single sound—a cicada buzzing above us, the bump of the music inside the club, a car pulling in. I had never had a panic attack before, but started to wonder if this was what it felt like. My hands were clammy. If I hadn't opened my mouth to speak, I probably would've forgotten to breathe.

Finn put his hand on my arm. "Calm down, okay?" I didn't realize I was squeezing the steering wheel. "It'll be all right. We're in this together."

"If I knew who the bastard was behind this, I'd run him over with my truck." I hated having my life turned so upside down and feeling helpless to right it again. All the suspects seemed to cast more doubt than provide answers, and I wasn't any closer to solving this case than when the day started. I was devoting more time to this craziness than to my livelihood, not getting anywhere, and it was really grinding on me.

"I don't doubt you would. Maybe you should let me drive?" Finn offered with a smile. I relaxed a little. I knew he was half joking, but I took him up on his offer anyway. I tossed over my keys and we switched spots. Driving down Highway 17 is always creepy at night, anyway, even when you're not freaking out. I'd rather let someone else drive it any day.

9

A minute away from the clubs and, already, tall swamp oaks blocked out the stars, their long draping branches hiding whatever creatures lived in the shadows. Whenever I'd pass through here at night, it always seemed safer driving down the center of the road, away from the darkness.

Flickers of white caught my eye to the right and stole my attention. Focusing, I realized they were the white wooden crosses of a Baptist cemetery. *Oh goody, another reminder of death.* I couldn't help it; I was freaking out again. My skin began itching from nerves. Hives would break out if I didn't relax. Calming breaths didn't seem to help, but maybe locking the door would. My hand searched in the darkness for the lock. I pushed it down and scooted along the bench seat toward Finn. The truck windows were still down, but I didn't want to roll them up. The sound of the wind rushing into the cab made up for our silence. Finn wrapped his arm around my shoulder, and I felt protected.

"Don't take this the wrong way, but do you want to stay at my place tonight?" Finn asked.

I knew what he meant. With murder on both our minds, neither one of us wanted to sleep alone. "Sure. That'll probably be the only way I'll sleep tonight." Finn nodded his head in agreement, leaving it at that, and continued to drive back to downtown Port Haven.

Back at the marina, Finn parked my truck, and I got out to walk around to the driver's side, figuring we were just stopping for him to pick up his truck. "So, do you want me to follow you to your place?" I asked.

Finn smirked. "Sure, but we're already here." I looked around and wondered where *here* meant exactly. Naturally, I scanned the docks. Finn followed my eyes and said, "I wish. I live right there." He pointed to the second story of Murphy's. *The bait shop? Well, that could be cool.* At least he had water views.

We walked around the side of Murphy's and down the boardwalk, arriving at the same spot where I had spent most of the afternoon before standing in the sun. Only this time, we didn't hang out next to the ice cooler. Instead, I followed Finn up a set of newly refurbished wooden stairs. Every other grayed step had been replaced. The guardrail also looked new; it lacked that weathered, splintered look you'd expect for being so close to the water.

At the top of the stairs, Finn unlocked the door and reached his arm around on the inside wall for the light switch. Soft yellow light brought the interior into focus. The loft-style apartment opened into the kitchen. The walls were painted a warm white, and the appliances had that retro, fifties look. Cans of Coke were stacked on the counter next to the sink. From what I could tell, the kitchen was the only outdated part of the place. Like the stairs, a newly constructed wooden breakfast bar separated the kitchen from the living room. Two oversized windows overlooked the docks, inviting plenty of natural light in. Even at night, the large flat-screen television hanging on the wall was visible.

Finn turned on a floor lamp in the living room and gave me a quick tour, which basically required me to spin around in a circle. Besides housing the television, the living room was furnished with a brown leather sofa and matching recliner. The furniture reminded me of a nice pair of jeans that were worn in all the right places. A coffee table, similar in design to the breakfast bar with a poured-gray cement top, was centered in front of the seating area. The walls didn't offer much in decoration, unless you counted roped fishing nets as art.

Off the living room, was Finn's bedroom. It looked like he had stacked dark-stained wooden crates to section off the space and offer privacy. The bedroom lacked a door, but it's not like he needed one, seeing that he lived alone. The only problem was the front windows. I imagined the sunrise would be brutal.

Finn spun me to the right and pointed out the bathroom. I was relieved to see *that* room had a door. The three Cokes I had at the club had worked their way to my bladder, and I really had to pee. I excused myself and headed for the loo.

Like his truck, Finn's bathroom was clean. The toilet seat was down too. *Now that's impressive.* The room was small, with just enough space for a sink, toilet, and standing shower, but everything looked new. It seemed Finn had been busy with renovations. I couldn't resist and peeked inside his medicine cabinet, but it was empty. *How disappointing.* At least my reflection didn't look too bad. That twelve-hour lipstick really did last, which made me think, *Beauty Secrets does offer a men's line. I should hook Finn up with a few free samples and see what he thinks. I bet his deck hands would love the ultra-moisturizing hand cream, even if they would never admit to it. In fact, they could use the entire moisturizing line with built in SPF, the way the sun beats down on them all day.*

The marina really was an untapped market. I could expand my business to a whole new set of clientele if I could just get Finn on board. I shuffled that thought to the back of my mind with a promise to myself to ask Finn about it later.

When I walked out of the bathroom, Finn was sitting on the edge of the coffee table watching the television. Stepping closer, I saw that it was a rerun of the eleven o'clock news. An anchor reported on the Siebold case, while the screen cut to the footage from yesterday afternoon. It looked like the reporters had already linked Ann Marie's and Roger's murders. Watching the footage, I recognized Finn right away, but it took me a second to realize that I was standing next to him. My expression was empty, and my normal tan complexion was pasty, a sickly shade of greenish yellow. I looked horrible and hoped none of my clients recognized me.

Finn turned around and saw my face. "Sorry, I turned it on and there we were." He turned the channel and got up to walk toward me.

"It's okay. What did the news say? Anything new?" I asked.

"No, we still know more than they do." Finn walked past me to the kitchen and got two glasses of water. "Are you sure you're okay?" he asked.

"Yeah, I'm fine. I just think everything's finally sinking in and, to tell you the truth, it just pisses me off," I said.

"You surprise me. Most girls would be running away from all of this, but you want to charge right at it," Finn said.

"Well, it's not like I have much choice. Detective Brandle's too busy, so someone has to take over, do something." The detective hadn't returned one of my calls yet. "Besides, this is my life we're talking about. I'm not about to find a couple of dead bodies and let their killer get off scot-free. Let alone, allow a homicidal maniac to attack me again."

"I guess that's one way to look at it," he said.

"I'm not one to lie down and wait," I said.

"I didn't think you were," Finn replied before disappearing into his room. I plopped down on the couch, feeling spent. Finn returned, carrying a blanket, pillow, and a pair of sweat pants and a t-shirt.

"I know they're not your usual digs, but I didn't think you'd want to sleep in those jeans all night."

"No, that's awesome. Thanks. I appreciate it." I did a quick change in the bathroom and then settled in on the couch.

Finn had turned the channel and was relaxing in the recliner when I returned. I'd never been one to watch sports, especially the evening's highlights, but tonight they proved to be the perfect distraction. My eyelids grew heavy and I didn't fight it. I felt safe with Finn next to me and more than cozy cuddled up on his couch, wearing his comfy clothes. Relaxed and warm, I was out before the first commercial break.

I woke in the morning with my cheek squished against the leather arm of the couch. The pillow Finn had given me was tucked against my side. I picked my head up, peeling my cheek off the couch, and looked around for a clock. Green neon numbers glowed on the microwave display in the still-darkened kitchen. I wasn't surprised to see that it was just after seven. With these living room windows, I was amazed I had slept in this long. I was right; that morning sunrise was a killer.

I smoothed my dark hair back out of my face and formed a ponytail, but it was pointless without a hair tie. My locks fell back down my shoulders, and I tucked my bangs behind my ears.

Without getting up, I looked around the apartment for any sign of Finn, but all was quiet. Like a little kid, I got up and tiptoed over to the bedroom's crate walls and peered inside. His messy bed was empty. I spun around on my toes and looked over toward the bathroom, but the door was open and the light was off. I wasn't a very good detective. I had no idea where Finn had gone or when he had left.

Walking back to the couch, I spotted a clue on the breakfast bar. Next to a blueberry muffin was a note. *Sorry, had a fishing charter this morning. Hope you slept well. The coffee should still be hot. – Finn.*

Well, that was sweet. A mug with a fish decal and the saying *Gone Fishin'* was out on the counter next to the coffee pot. It wasn't a chai latte, but it was caffeine. I went to pour myself a mug when there was a knock at the front door.

"Finn, sweetie, you home?" a woman's voice asked.

I ducked down in the kitchen, even though there was no way the woman could see me. I prayed she didn't have a key. Even though nothing had happened between Finn and me, I didn't feel like trying to convince the mystery woman of that. In my experience, there's only one reason a woman spent the night with a man ... and it wasn't to watch sports.

The woman knocked again. I didn't move an inch.

"You there, babe? I *really* want to see you right now." Her voice purred through the door. I thought of Finn's comment yesterday at lunch, about no one else's toes to step on. *My ass,* I thought. He was such a liar! I was sure the mystery woman outside would agree, but I wasn't about to ask her. "Baby? If you can hear me, call me later. I've got plans for us. Hot, dirty plans."

Sweet sugar! I did not want to hear anymore.

I stayed crouched down, in case the woman was still out front, but she didn't say anything else. After a couple minutes, I stood back up. Well, didn't that just suck. Finn had a girlfriend, or someone he was sleeping with. Of course, he did. A guy that good looking never had to go too far for a piece of ass. If she was his girlfriend, it was a total game changer. Girls have a code of conduct, too, and I had crossed the line by staying over last night. If he was my boyfriend, I'd be ticked to find another woman at his place. I looked down at Finn's shirt and sweatpants, furious. *So much for Finn being a nice guy.* I felt like such an idiot. I should've never accepted his offer to check out the clubs with me. I should've taken Aria or Eric instead. Lesson learned.

I waited until I was sure the woman was back down the steps before getting dressed and gathering my things to head out the door. Downstairs, the ringing up of a sale made its way up through the floorboards, and I wondered if the woman had ever left after all.

MY PICKUP WAS SO warm and stuffy when I got in, that I had been focused on rolling down the windows and not reading the note stuck to the windshield. I tilted my head to read the words, *Let secrets lie or you will DIE.*

I thought, *Well, isn't that nice; it even rhymes.* The note was written in a child-like manner or by someone who had written with the opposite hand. I scrambled out of the car and pulled the note out from under my windshield wiper blade to examine it more closely. The handwriting creeped me out. It looked like it had been written in crayon, or maybe it was lipstick. I didn't touch the lettering for fear I would smear it or damage the evidence. Of course, I surveyed the parking lot, but no one suspicious jumped out at me. I didn't even peg anyone who could be Finn's girl-friend. The person who left the note was probably long gone after seeing my truck had been parked here all night. I thought about calling Aria, but she taught a sunrise yoga class (crazy, I know) and I already knew where Finn was, and I was in no hurry to talk to him. It was obvious who the real person I should call was. I just hoped this time he would finally answer his phone.

As luck would have it, Detective Brandle answered on the third ring. "Morning, Ms. Diaz," he said. His greeting caught me off guard. I guess I shouldn't be surprised that he recognized my number. I'd called him enough times in the past two days.

"Morning, Detective. Listen, sorry for calling you again, but someone left a creepy note on my car this morning. I'm pretty sure it has to do with the Seibold case. Have a minute to talk?"

"I can do that. Mind meeting me down at Sweet Thangs? I could use a cup of coffee," he said.

"Sounds great. I'll be there in five." *Looks like I get my chai latte after all.*

Sweet Thangs was busy for a Wednesday morning at eight o'clock. The shop's whimsical décor reminded me of Disney World, and the treats were just as magical. That wasn't all that brought locals to the shop. Next to their sugary confections, Sweet Thangs also brewed a mean cup of Joe and had the best chai latté in town. The frosted blue walls and white tabletops painted a summer scene that contradicted our planned topic of conversation. Patrons lined up along the counter and placed their orders for coffee, scones, and other sugary delights. The place was uncomfortably crowded, but the customers' chatter would help drown out our voices. Outside, customers sat on the wooden benches of the scattered two-tops, with their morning coffee and pastry of choice. Of course, I couldn't resist and ordered a cream-cheese-stuffed cinnamon roll to go with my latte. With the way my morning was going, I needed it. And did I mention it was stuffed with cream cheese? Seriously, who could resist? What can I say? I'm an emotional eater.

Detective Brandle had already staked out a table, and I soon joined him with my sugary, fat-packed breakfast, trying not to feel like a pig while he sipped his black coffee.

"Thanks for meeting me," I said. From the bags under the detective's eyes, I knew he'd rather be in bed. Why men didn't wear makeup was beyond me. At least he wasn't wearing the same black pants and white shirt that I had come to associate as his uniform. No, today he was less formal - khaki shorts and a navy Polo shirt. Maybe it was his day off.

"That looks good," Detective Brandle said, eying my roll.

"It is. You should totally have one," I said.

"The misses would hound me until the Fourth of July if she saw me eating that. My sugar's been up," the detective explained.

"Ah." Yeah, this definitely wasn't a smart breakfast choice if you were watching your sugar intake. I'd have to make some serious dietary changes if my sugar ever got out of whack.

"So, what have you found?" Detective Brandle asked, getting right to the point.

I told him about the note, and what I learned at The Palms the night before. I also told him about the Siebold's son, Philip, and what Mrs. J.'s theory was. I thought about bringing up Marion and her alleged affair with the good doctor, but held my tongue. There was only so much gossip I was willing to spread around. Until I saw some proof of Marion and Dr. Michelson's relationship, I was keeping my mouth shut. Besides, the way Roger doted on Ann Marie, I figured Marion deserved a tryst or two.

Detective Brandle turned serious. "I'm not sure what this note's all about, but you've got to be careful. Back off and let us work this case."

"Yeah, but—" I began to protest.

"No. Listen, I can add extra patrols to your area, but you need to be smart. Do you have someone you can stay with?" he asked.

Aria came to mind first, but I would hate myself if something happened to her or, heaven forbid, Arjun, because of me. The murderer seemed to be getting nervous. They'd already killed two people in one week, plus assaulting and now threatening me. Who knew what else they would do? I was staying as far away from Aria as possible.

Finn's place could've been an option, but not anymore. Not until I figured out who the mystery woman was. Of course, there was always my parents' condo. They'd be away for the remainder of the week, which reminded me, I needed to get my butt over there and water the plants before they all croaked.

"I have some options," I told Detective Brandle.

"Well, you should take a serious look at them. Maybe even get out of town for a couple of days, and keep your eyes open. If you see anyone or anything suspicious, call nine-one-one immediately," he said.

"Will do," I said automatically.

"We should also look at your windshield for prints. Maybe we'll get lucky. I'll have the note processed too," he said.

"My prints are probably all over it," I said.

"Possibly, but we can still take a look. If we find something, we can always rule yours out," he said.

"Okay." That made sense. I showed Detective Brandle where I had parked, and stood back to let him do his work. The process wasn't nearly as technical as I thought it would be, although, he did wear rubber gloves while handling the note and checking for prints. I watched as he shined his flashlight through my windshield and then dusted the area where I said the note had been found.

"Bingo! Looks like we got a couple prints. Maybe a thumb and index finger," Detective Brandle said.

I looked at the print he found on the wiper blade. "Shouldn't be mine. I pulled the note off from the corner." And, I didn't regularly go around adjusting my wiper blades.

Detective Brandle worked to lift the print, using his credit card to smooth out the tape and cleanly transfer the print to it. It was a trick he said he'd learned years ago. He then peeled off the tape and affixed it to an index-looking card, jotting down a couple notes on it when he finished.

"It will take a while to get this processed. Don't expect to hear back on this any time soon. It would be nice to find a match though, give us a starting point."

I agreed that it would be. Maybe a print would match the others lifted from Roger's house or boat.

"In the meantime, you be careful. Like I said, call nine-one-one if it's an emergency, and call me if you hear of anything else," he said.

"Got it." I think Detective Brandle was going to say something else but, like usual, his cell phone rang.

"Brandle," the detective said almost with a sigh. "Again? You've got to be kidding me. When? No. I'm nearby. On it."

I listened to a bit more of the conversation than was probably polite to, but I couldn't help it. Detective Brandle signed off with a couple choice swear words, and it was enough for me to get the general gist.

"Another break in?" I asked.

"The Chocolatier. This is ridiculous. Who robs a candy shop at nine o'clock in the morning?"

"Wow," I mouthed. The Chocolatier was known for their fancy-schmancy chocolates, like lavender-infused truffles and gold-foiled petit fours.

"The day just keeps getting better." Detective Brandle looked at his phone. "Listen, I've got to run, but I'll be in touch. Remember, keep your eyes out and don't hesitate to call emergency services if you need to."

I promised Detective Brandle I would be smart and extra vigilant, and waved him off. Getting into the truck, I took a moment to check my emotions. While I was happy to have finally caught up with Detective Brandle, there was still a mound of dread in my stomach. With the robberies now happening in broad daylight, I doubted he'd have any extra time to devote to the case. Looked like I was still on my own.

$\mathcal{P}$epper spray, a baseball bat, and a hunting knife lined the counter at the sporting goods store. I thought about purchasing a handgun too, but I didn't have a clue of how to use one. The salesman was very helpful and suggested I rent a couple at the gun range to get a feel for what I liked. That sounded like a smart idea, and safer than my original plan of just going with the meanest-looking one I could find that would still fit in my purse. I could just see myself getting knocked on my butt the first time I fired it. It looked like Aria and I would be hitting up the gun range this weekend. Come to think of it, she might already own a handgun. Her late husband was a big-time collector of ... well, everything.

I paid for my items, put the pepper spray on my key chain, the knife in my beauty bag, the baseball bat on the passenger seat, and pulled out of the parking lot to head to my parents' condo. At least their place had security. Well, that is, if you counted old man Miles as a security guard. He was nosey enough for the job, that was for sure, but I was pretty sure he lacked the physical strength to stop a determined toddler, let alone a madman. That was okay because, while Miles kept an eye out, I'd provide the heat, if necessary.

I eyed my defense arsenal on the passenger seat. No one could say I wasn't taking precautions.

Pulling into my parents' complex, there seemed to be a yard sign on every corner. They read things such as *It's no SECRET ... Justine is the best in beauty,* and *All you need is Justine.* If I had a permanent marker, I might've crossed it all out and wrote in: *For a good time, call...* Alas, I was sans a marker.

I looked up the street and smiled. Inez was unmistakable, wearing the bright purple sunhat she won at the beauty demo. It sat perfectly straight, weightless, atop her brown nest of hair. She carried a stack of Justine's signs under her arm, having yanked them out of the ground. *Bless her.* I parked the pickup at the end of my parents' driveway and walked over to meet her. She stood, ripping the signs in half so they would fit into her recycling bin.

"I don't know who this Justine girl is, but she looks like trouble. She is, isn't she? I can sense it," Inez said.

"She is," I replied.

"Well, it's a good thing I told her to skedaddle then, and to take her signs with her. Here I am, just trying to work on my flowers, and she comes up to me and starts bad-mouthing you. Can you believe that?"

I could. Looked like my attorney needed to send a more forceful letter, too.

"Good riddance. And if she's smart, she won't come back. But she's not smart, is she? No, I know she's not. She wouldn't be putting up signs like this in our neighborhood if she was. She was probably at that beauty demo of yours too. Am I right?"

I nodded to confirm she was right.

"Trash, that's what she is. But not you. You're a real beauty, inside and out."

Inez was too kind. I was thinking I was more of a hot mess than a beauty. I had yet to take a proper shower since the night before, and I was feeling less than stellar.

"But look at me, I'm a total mess," she continued. "I had to get out here and tend to my plants before it got too hot. These wild geraniums overgrow my sunscape daisies every year." Inez motioned to the ground for me to see the wilting geraniums she had pulled. They didn't look like weeds to me. That showed how much I knew about gardening. Folks who cared about their plants kept them far away from me. Just ask my parents. I was pretty sure their plants were as good as dead by now.

"They don't mess with my hydrangea or purple coneflowers, though, see? They know. They know who they can mess with." Inez pointed across the way at two plants. If she hadn't used the word purple to describe one of them, I wouldn't have known which was which.

"Those wild geraniums are smart. They only sprout up next to the weaker plants, like my daisies. Maybe I'll pot them instead. Take them right out of the ground. You have style. What do you think?"

I went to answer, but Inez just kept on talking.

"Terracotta always looks so classy; that's what I think. Oh, but I used white porcelain out back and they should match, don't you think? You must be careful with terracotta, too, you know. One cold winter night and, crack, your pot's ruined. I'll have to think about this. I've got room on the back porch for another flower pot or two, that's for sure. It would open this front space right up. I could plant a peony right here." She pointed to where the daisies were. "They have such beautiful flowers." Inez looked at the spot, as if picturing the peonies in her head. "Oh, but the ants," she said, quickly changing her mind. "I can't have peonies so close to the front door. You know how ants love peonies. It's not just those little ones, but those big, black nasty carpenter ants. That would be a disaster. Maybe I could plant chrysanthemum instead. Don't you think that would be lovely?"

This time, Inez paused for an answer, and I had no idea what to say. It would help if I knew what chrysanthemums were. I found myself nodding and agreeing with what she was saying anyway, "Yeah, you're right. That would look nice." Clients tended to like it when you agreed with them, and Inez seemed to have thought all this through.

"Good heavens. Listen to me, gabbing away about my plants when you've had such a horrible week. How you holding up, dear? And poor Marion, how's she doing? The whole town is just buzzing with the news. A double homicide? I can't believe it. My grandson wants me to come stay with him; but, why should I? No one's going to bother me. I'm perfectly safe right here."

I was pretty sure Inez was safe, but maybe not if I crashed at my parents' condo right across the street. The more I thought about it, the more it seemed like the safest place for me to stay, for everyone's sake, was my place. Plus, if I stayed at my parents' place, I'd have to stay inside all the time or run the risk of bumping into Inez and being late to everything. I ran late enough on my own. It would be a nightmare. Inez kept on talking, which only served to make up my mind. I was absolutely, one hundred percent going back to my apartment after this.

I mentally checked back into the conversation to hear Inez say, "That's Tico for you, always looking out for his

Grams. He's such a sweet man. I just can't believe he hasn't settled down yet."

Inez's eyes sparkled, and I knew exactly where this conversation was going.

"Ziva, you're single, aren't you? You should really meet Tico. Dark hair, brown eyes, he's a looker," she said.

He did sound nice, but it was bad form to start dating clients' relatives. If the relationship turned sour, you could kiss your client goodbye. And with the way Inez talked, I could only imagine what she'd be saying about me. Plus, after my morning, I felt like I already had one too many potential men in my life. Finn was still on my list.

"Thanks, but I'm not looking right now. I'll let you know if I change my mind." I hoped she wasn't offended.

"Suit yourself. Hey, I know what I was going to ask you about. Do you sell any of that rejuvenating cream? I don't think I can keep these crow's feet back much longer. I was thinking about the Q-10 formula, or those peptides, or was it antioxidants? Which one is the best? Have you tried them out? Of course, you haven't. Just look at your skin. It's so beautiful. When I was a young girl like yourself, I had beautiful skin too. I used to think, *Inez, you have beautiful skin*, and I did. Next to my dimples it was one of my best features." And just like that, Inez was off on a different tangent again.

∾

Sweet sugar, could Inez talk. I had no idea if she was hyped up about something, or if she always talked liked that. I never did get the opportunity to tell her that I'd be delivering her order in the next day or so. After discussing every rejuvenating cream, mask, and serum that Beauty

Secrets sold, the conversation switched from baking (again, no help there), to knitting (yeah, no knitting needles here), to playing bridge (I didn't have a clue). Inez went on and on about how much she loved the card game and how much she hoped tomorrow's match wouldn't be canceled. Turned out, they were one player short and, as Inez said, "You *have* to have four players to play." I was on my toes and waiting with my excuse when she asked me to join them. I'll do a lot to earn client business, but a girl has to draw the line somewhere. When Aria called to invite me to lunch a minute later, it was a welcome interruption.

"WHAT'S UP, girlie? Where've you been?" Aria asked when we met up. We sat outside on the front deck of Maxine's, waiting for our food to arrive. I had ordered a double cheeseburger with a chocolate martini on the side. Aria went with something much lighter—grilled salmon with a spring salad and ice water. We both tried not to make a face when the other ordered.

"You wouldn't believe my life right now. I've had so much drama, it's ridiculous. If it's not being attacked or finding another dead body, it's dealing with Justine, or being threatened by some psycho." I filled Aria in on the note.

"That's crazy, girl. What did the police say?" Aria asked.

"Detective Brandle says he's got it under control, but I don't buy it. Not with the crazy robberies going on."

"I know. What's up with that? It's freaking me out," she said.

"I know, right?" I said.

"So, now what?" Aria asked.

"Now I need to figure out what to do next," I said.

"You can stay with me and Arjun until you figure it out. You know that, right?" she said.

"Thanks, but I don't want to drag you guys into this. I thought about crashing at my parents' place, but I really don't want to do that either." Like I said, not only could I put Inez in danger, but I'd run the risk of running into her at the mailbox every morning, and being twenty minutes late to every appointment. Imagine how happy that'd make Mrs. J.

"No, I've only got a few more days until they're home, and I'm praying this is all cleared up by then," I said.

"It sounded on the news like the police had some good leads..." Aria was trying to be positive.

"I wish. Eric made that part up."

"Shoot, I was hoping it wasn't something like that. You know, I still think the police should be considering Marion," she said.

"I know, but come on. Marion? I keep going back to it, but I can't see her killing her husband. Divorce? Yes. Murder? No way," I said.

"Girlie, no one knows what goes on in a marriage, other than the two people in it. Who knows what went on behind their closed doors? Marion may act all sweet, sipping lemonade on her front porch, but she could have a temper like the devil. I mean, how well do you ever really know someone?"

That last comment really hit home. If my ex-fiancé hadn't slipped up and accidentally swapped our phones before deleting his sexting, who knows when I would've discovered his affair? I could've married the bastard. Sweet sugar, was my Nan looking out for me on that one. Although I would've appreciated it if she would've intervened a little bit sooner. Saved me some heartache and the down payment on a gorgeous dress.

"Well, lookie there," Aria said. On cue, Dr. Michelson and Marion walked up the entrance to Maxine's. The doctor opened the door for Marion and put his hand on her back to guide her in. Something about the action seemed more than a friendly, *Here let me get the door for you.* Marion looked fresh-faced and a little too happy to be a grieving wife. Midnight Noir mascara covered her every lash, and her pout looked perfect, courtesy of the Plum Pastry lipstick I had dropped off earlier in the week.

"Seriously?" I asked.

"You know I want to say told you so," Aria said.

I sipped my martini and watched Marion and Dr. Michelson through the front windows as they slipped into a back booth. Their seating preference only added to my suspicion.

"It definitely looks like there's a little something going on there," Aria said.

"I hate to admit it, but I think you're right," I said.

"Now what?" Aria asked.

"Well, we can't eavesdrop from over here, and I highly doubt they're going to start making out." Maybe I was wrong. Dr. Michelson took that moment to reach across the table for Marion's hand. He wasn't shy in the touchy-feely department. Marion looked around before accepting it. I wondered what she would do if I walked right over and said hi. That thought left me inspired. I took a gulp of my martini and headed their way to find out.

"Pssst, Ziva, where are you going?" Aria knew exactly where I was going. I ignored her and slid inside through the side serving door.

I wasn't trying to sneak up on them, per se, but the look on Marion's face was priceless when I popped up and said, "Hi, Marion." Her blue eyes flashed with alarm and she dropped Dr. Michelson's hand like a hot coal. The doctor reached for her hand once more, but Marion withdrew it and folded her hands on her lap. It looked like Marion wasn't as eager as Dr. Michelson to go public with their relationship.

"Marion, Dr. Michelson, how's it going?" I asked.

Marion looked around to see who else I was with. "Fine, I'm doing just fine." Her eyes continued to dart around the restaurant. "Rich here helped me around the house today, and I offered to take him out to lunch as a thank you. We're old friends, you know."

I wasn't sure I bought that, but I smiled politely and said, "That's nice of you. I'm just having lunch with a girlfriend of mine, but I can help you out afterward if you need a hand." It wasn't nice of me, but I enjoyed seeing Marion squirm.

Dr. Michelson took the lead. "I don't think that's such a good idea. I heard about the attack, and I really think you should be taking it easy." Marion looked grateful to be saved from having to come up with an excuse.

Dr. Michael's comment gave me an idea. "You know, the paramedic said I should follow up with you, but I just really haven't had the time. Maybe I'll call tomorrow and see if I can get in to see you." I massaged my neck for emphasis. I was betting I could get more out of the doctor if we talked one-on-one.

"That'd be a good idea. Give Sandy a call. I'm sure she'll get you in right away," he said.

"Okay, thanks, Doc." The waitress started to make her way over with their drink order. "Well, you two enjoy your lunch. Marion, I'll probably stop by in the next day or so with the rest of your order, if that's all right." I had been waiting on a couple of backorders to be shipped, including Marion's foundation.

Marion nodded that it was okay. I could tell she was still uncomfortable with the situation, which only fueled my speculation. "I'll see you both soon then," I said and walked away.

"You're bad," Aria said in between mouthfuls. Our food had been delivered in my absence, and my cheeseburger looked divine.

"What? If Marion and Dr. Michelson don't want to be seen in public together, then they shouldn't be out to lunch holding hands."

"That's true. So, what did they say?"

"Not much. Marion mumbled something about them being old friends and her treating him to lunch. I could tell she wanted to hide under the table, or make me disappear."

"I'll bet," Aria said.

"Dr. Michelson, on the other hand, didn't seem so shy. Not sure what that's all about. I'm hoping to learn more at my doctor's appointment."

"You getting sick?"

"Don't have to. Follow up appointment." I pointed to my neck.

"Brilliant. Can I come with?"

"Of course. You might catch something I miss."

"Excellent. This will be fun." Aria was just as excited as me for a trip to the doctor's office.

After lunch, Aria and I parted ways. Even though I would've loved spending the rest of the day hanging out, with our schedules, it just wasn't possible. Aria had to pick Arjun up from karate and I had a run to get in, not to mention some beauty business to take care of. *Note to self: don't eat a cheeseburger and drink a martini and then attempt go for a run—ever.* If dehydration doesn't kill you, the stomach cramps will. Of course, I knew it was stupid to work out after lunch, but I felt like I was seriously slacking in the physical health department, especially giving in to all my cravings lately.

Sweaty and slightly nauseous, I left the park's running trail and headed to the UPS Store to pick up my product shipment. Today, I had skipped working out at the beach. Regardless of how beautiful the scenery was, I didn't feel like running into Finn. I still wasn't sure how to address what had happened earlier today. After that, I stopped by Ruffles, the clothing boutique downtown, and stocked up on some leggings and flowy shirts. I was looking a bit more voluptuous than usual, which I didn't mind, but I needed some new clothes to match the curves. Besides, after today's horrendous run, I decided exercise was overrated.

Back home, as I sat and organized my products, I felt a bit jumpy. Twice, I got up and peered out the living room window at the street below, each time pulling the drapes tighter. I hated that eerie feeling of being watched. It was the same sensation I had that night at the restaurant. I double checked that my front door was locked, and closed all the blinds before settling down with the baseball bat at my side. Anyone who knew me knew I wasn't afraid to use it either.

I spent some time organizing my desk, filing invoices, reordering Beauty Secrets gift bags and switching out my demo bag, leaving the hunting knife in the side pocket, of course. Last season's catalogs littered the floor until I stacked them up under the desk with a promise to recycle them instead of chucking them out. I didn't need to worry about the remaining free samples I'd found going to waste. Red lipstick never went out of style.

I pulled out my phone and went through my calendar. The city's spring wedding expo was already coming up this Saturday. I was so unprepared, but I was not going to skip it.

I'd bet my weight in chocolate Justine would be there. A fair amount of money could be made doing makeup for brides and their entourages, and I honestly loved weddings, and not just for the cake. No, I had to go to the expo. I quickly jumped back online and doubled my sample order and updated my wedding-season-package flyer.

Just when I was ready to call it an early night, my cell phone rang, scaring the life out of me. My first thought was that it was Finn, and I wasn't sure if I wanted to answer it. I was surprised to see it was Eric; and better yet, he wanted to have dinner tonight. There was no point in staying home all night, scaring myself silly, and dinner with Eric did sound nice. So, I readily accepted.

RED ALWAYS BROUGHT out my dark features and made me feel sexy. Aria's red sleeveless coat dress was no exception and, courtesy of my newfound curves, I was looking extra fabulous. I borrowed the dress a couple beauty demos ago and hadn't returned it yet. I debated wearing it. After all, it was a little hubba hubba, and I wasn't sure that was the look I was going for. In fact, I had a moment of panic on the way to the restaurant. What was I doing meeting Eric for dinner? But then, I reminded myself it was just dinner. Completely casual and no need to freak out about it. I was only exploring my options, like trying on new lipsticks until I found the one shade I loved, and we all know how difficult that can be—mattes, gloss, reds, nudes—need I go on?

I pulled up to Midori's Sushi just after 7 p.m. and saw Eric sitting at a table alongside the window. He was wearing a dark blue dress shirt and gray slacks. Even without a tie, he looked classy. *Dang, that man can dress.* I was happy I had gone with the red dress, and smoothed the fabric out as I walked inside to greet him.

"Ziva, you look beautiful." Eric stood and gave me a quick kiss on the cheek. I thanked him for the compliment and sat across from him. On the table was a white candle in a frosted-glass container, along with the dinner menu and drink specials. I didn't need to look at either menu to know I wanted a lychee fruit martini and the dragon roll. The sweetness of the drink and spiciness of the roll was a favorite combination of mine.

"So, what is it about investing that you find so appealing?" I asked Eric, while waiting for our dinner to arrive.

"I don't know if you know, but I didn't come from much."

"Never would guess." Eric seemed like the type who'd been born with a silver spoon in his mouth.

"Yeah, well, it's not something I go around telling a lot of people," he said with a smile. "It's just that I always wanted to become more, have more. That's what I've worked toward most of my life."

"You're driven."

"To make money," Eric added.

I could understand that, but wasn't sure I agreed with it. I favored the finer things in life too, but money wasn't my top priority. I mean, hello, I was a beauty consultant. That didn't mean that I didn't have any goals. My motivators were just different.

"And you met Roger..." I questioned.

"When he was looking for someone to join his firm. He needed someone with strong drive and an aptitude for finance. I met both requirements. I just needed Roger's knowledge and guidance to take it to the next level. Together, we did just that."

"What is it about you and the beauty business? Well,

besides the obvious." I smiled in an aren't-you-cute way and took a drink of my martini to hopefully keep myself from blushing.

"Honestly, I love making people feel good about themselves. When you take the time to pamper yourself or treat yourself to that special lipstick, nail polish, or whatever, you're saying to yourself, 'I'm worth it. I deserve some *me* time. I want to look my best for myself, no one else.' The way a person feels about herself ... or himself...," I said with a smile, "can be empowering. I want my clients to feel empowered."

"That's admirable," Eric said.

"I like to think so. Someday, I'd love to take it to the next level too. Open my own shop and eventually develop my own products. I could probably get a good deal on a commercial building downtown right now," I said. *Especially if the robberies and breaks-ins keep happening.*

"If you're serious about the business aspect of it, I could help you with the financing, show you how the backend of it works and put you in contact with a couple potential investors."

I wondered if Eric could see the stars in my eyes. "That would be amazing." My mind was already racing ahead, putting together a business plan and designing my brand. Now more than ever, this killer needed to be caught so I could move on with my life.

"This week has been something, hasn't it?" Eric said.

"It has," I agreed.

"I hate the way we met, but I'm glad we did," he said.

"Me too."

"So, I propose a toast. To us. To new opportunities," he said.

"To opportunities. Cheers." That was something I could definitely drink to.

We spent the rest of dinner talking about everything and nothing at the same time. Well, Eric did. I mostly listened. I learned that Eric would be a heck of a business partner, and I could see why Roger had brought him on board. I was excited to see what he could do for my potential new business. However, in the relationship department, he was a dud. We just had too many different priorities. I was all about helping people feel good about themselves and making a difference. Eric was about money and ... well, money. I had a feeling I was more into the way he dressed than the person he was under the clothes. It was a total bummer because he really was smart and good looking. I knew that wasn't enough though. I had already had one disaster of a relationship and really wasn't looking for another. *Look at me, being all smart. Perhaps I have grown up a bit.*

So, while Eric may have been a no-go in the dating department, he was definitely someone I wanted to keep in my rolodex.

11

I called Sandy Thompson, the friendliest receptionist in town, the next morning to make my appointment with Dr. Michelson. It turned out, she had an eleven o'clock opening that morning, which I was happy to take. Aria taught a yoga class at the same time, so I knew she wouldn't be able to make it, but I scheduled the appointment anyway. I was going in alone.

I left my apartment shortly after ten-thirty and headed downtown, toward the historic district, to Dr. Michelson's office. Most of the homes in the area used to belong to prominent southern families in the early nineteen-hundreds, but have since been converted into retail spaces, like Sweet Thangs next door to the office. I debated stopping at the sweet shop before my appointment, for a chai latte, but somehow managed to bypass their parking lot and pull into the doctor's instead. Maybe I was learning a little bit of willpower. Or, maybe I just didn't like being late.

Dr. Michelson's office couldn't have been more welcoming. Throughout the years, the furniture may have been updated and magazines replaced, but the office still held the same warm ambiance. Clusters of oversized reading chairs were grouped together, around coffee tables stacked with children's books and magazines. A flowering hibiscus tree soaked in the South Carolina sun, peeking through the front bay window. On the opposite wall, a large fish tank, filled with yellow tangs and blue damsels, took up several feet. Coastal paintings and decorative seashells on the tables coordinated perfectly with the crisp, pale-blue walls and virgin oak floors. It was like visiting a friend's seaside home, as opposed to a doctor's office.

Even the reception desk was welcoming. Instead of a sliding glass window with a check-in pad, the office had a half-walled counter, where Sandy greeted and registered patients. Sandy was old when I was a little girl, and probably should've retired years ago, but she was one of those people who loved her job through and through.

"Good morning, Ziva. How's your folks doing?" she asked.

"Good. They're on a cruise right now for their anniversary," I said.

"Are they really? I've asked the mister to take me on a cruise a time or two, but he won't have it. You know how he feels about boats." I had no idea how Mr. Thompson felt about boats, but I nodded anyway. "Well tell them I said hi, and go ahead and take a seat. Doctor's running a little late," Sandy added.

That was unusual. Doctor Michelson rarely ran behind. I know, a rarity among today's medical professions, but that was one of the things I liked about him. He was always on time. I promised Sandy I'd pass on her hello, and took a seat at one of the comfy reading chairs to peruse the magazines. Nothing looked interesting enough to read, and I was starting to get mighty bored scrolling through my phone, when Dr. Michelson appeared at the door and invited me to follow him on back. Yet another abnormality. I wondered where his nurse, Kathy, was. I didn't see her anywhere. Maybe Dr. Michelson was just as eager to talk to me as I was to him.

The rooms on this side of the door looked much more like a traditional doctor's office. The dreaded scale stood next to the nurses' station. Evidence of pharmaceutical reps' visits appeared in the form of pens, tissue boxes, and pamphlets scattered along the station's counter. Tops of brightly labeled files peeked out from wall-mounted file holders, and each one of the examining rooms lining the hall had a gold number, like an address, affixed to its door. We stopped at room number two, and I went in and had a seat on top of the paper-covered table.

"So, how have you been feeling?" Doctor Michelson asked me. I didn't answer. I was too busy staring at the Plum Pastry lipstick stain on his lips. I didn't mean to gawk, but I could swear he'd been kissing Marion. That was her favorite shade. Sensing my scrutiny, Dr. Michelson wiped his mouth with the back of his hand, destroying any possible evidence.

"I'm doing all right," I finally managed to say. "My neck's been a little sore though."

"Let's take a look then," he said.

I breathed in and out, and turned my head side to side, like he asked me to, and answered his questions. No, I hadn't been feeling dizzy. No, I didn't have any problems with my vision. Yes, I was sleeping well. The whole time Dr. Michelson examined me, I was doing the same. Was that Marion's perfume I smelled on him or just my imagination? Did his shirt look a little wrinkled? Doctor Michelson gave me an odd sort of look, and I tried to play off my scrutiny by pretending to have something in my eye. It was totally lame, but the doctor didn't call me out on it, so maybe he bought it.

"Marion seems to be doing well, doesn't she?" I asked while he finished up his assessment.

"I wouldn't expect any different. Marion's a strong woman. She'll make it through this." Dr. Michelson said all this while writing a few notes down in my chart.

"You really think she'll be okay?" I asked.

"Okay? I think, in time, she'll be far better than okay. Roger put her through hell and honestly, I can't say I'm sorry he's dead."

Well, there was an honest answer if I ever heard one.

"If Roger was so rotten to her, then why did Marion stay married to him?" It was the one question that I kept coming back to. I had to ask it.

For a second, I thought Dr. Michelson was going to answer me, but he changed his mind. "I'll leave that up to Marion to answer. Right now, I wouldn't be too worried about her. She has good friends, good family, and we're all here for her," he said.

"Her son—," I said.

"Is in town," Dr. Michelson finished my sentence. "And if anyone can help her through this, it's him."

He's in town? Boy, would I like to meet him.

Before I could ask another question, Dr. Michelson brought the subject back around to the matter at hand. "Now, as for you, the muscles in your neck feel a little tight. Ibuprofen should help. You can also use ice or heat packs, whichever feel better, as necessary. Call if you have any new symptoms, and we'll get you in right away," he said.

"Thanks, Doc," I replied.

"You're really lucky. You know that, kiddo?" That was

one way to look at it. "So is Marion. She's just doesn't know it yet," he said.

I wanted to ask what he meant exactly, but the doctor already had one foot out the door. Luck wasn't an adjective I'd use to describe someone who just had their husband murdered in her home.

"Take care, and call Sandy if your pain worsens. If you get any numbness or radiating pain, we'll look at scheduling some tests; but if not, you should be fine. Just give it time to heal," he continued.

Before I could reply, he slipped the rest of the way out the door, and I was left with more questions than answers.

I LEFT Dr. Michelson's feeling restless. Inside, I knew the real person I wanted to talk to was Marion; but I wasn't sure how to approach the topic. I needed to be smart about it. No matter what I thought, getting choked out in her kitchen didn't make me privy to her sex life or the secrets of her marriage, but that was exactly what I wanted to talk to her about.

The right conversation starter still eluded me when I turned down her street and saw a silver BMW backing out of her driveway. I hung back a minute, giving the man time to pull out and drive off, before pulling in. Marion was sitting on the porch swing, looking blissfully content for once. I'd like to think it was the sapphire eyeliner she was wearing that made her eyes sparkle like that, but I knew better.

"I take it that was your son?" I said.

"You know Philip?" Marion seemed surprised.

"No, but I heard he was in town."

"He is, and it's so good to have him home. I can't tell you how much of a help he's already been."

Marion started to get teary-eyed, and I hoped she wasn't about to cry. I really, really hated to see people cry. It rated about a ten out of ten on the uncomfortable factor.

"Right now, he's headed down the police station to try and get some answers," she continued. "I told him they'd call us if they knew anything, but he couldn't wait that long. That's Philip for you." It sounded as if Philip was as restless as his mom.

"It sounds like you've missed him," I said.

"You have no idea. Roger never got it, and heaven knows Philip didn't care for him. Not that I blamed him."

"But you? He had to miss you." At that comment, Marion did start to cry. *Crap.* I stood there for a minute thinking about what I should do before deciding to just go with it. *If she's already an emotional mess...*

"I hate to say it, but your life seems better without Roger in it," I said.

Marion gave a little hysterical laugh. "It is. It really is. How awful is that?"

"I'm not sure it's awful, but it does make me wonder why it had to come to this for you to realize it. I mean, why didn't you two split years ago?"

"Believe me, I would've loved to, but I just couldn't," Marion said.

"What do you mean? Did you have like a crazy prenuptial agreement or something?" It was really the only thing I could think of.

"No, and even if we did, nothing as trivial as money could've kept me married to that man."

"Well what was it then? I don't understand."

"I'm sick. Did you know that?" Marion asked.

"I do. Well, I didn't, until recently; but now that I know, I'm sorry." I was surprised by the shift in conversation. I tried to follow where this was going.

"That's okay. Truthfully, I didn't want people to know. I wanted to go about living my life as normal as possible, but that became harder to do last year."

"What happened?" I asked.

"My cancer spread, and I was at stage four. Heaven knows I was so fed up with Roger and ready to walk away, but I couldn't. Not when I depended on him for so much."

"Roger was really there for you?" I asked.

"No, not at all. But his insurance was. I had no idea what would happen to my coverage if we separated. I couldn't chance it."

"I'd never thought of that." Something so simple, yet so important kept Marion married to Roger. It made perfect sense. Marion was a much stronger person than me. I wouldn't be able to face the public scrutiny or the lies with nearly half the dignity she projected. I could see why she had to though. What an awful situation to be in. The thought of Roger cheating on his wife while she battled cancer was disgusting and heartbreaking. It felt like the ultimate betrayal. Hurting your wife when she was at her weakest, for your own selfish pleasure. Roger was scum. I thought back to the girls at the strip club and how much they said Roger doted on Ann Marie. If you asked me, he should've spent more time doting on his wife, the one he took vows with, and not some stripper. Shame on Ann Marie, too. I don't care what the man was showering her with, she should've respected his wife and kept to a look-but-don't-touch policy. Neither one of them rated all that high on my moral meter.

"How are you feeling now?" I asked Marion.

"Well, the cancer seems to be in remission, if that's what you're asking. Of course, I had to have a double mastectomy and some lymph nodes removed, but I'm healing."

"That's good."

"Rich, Dr. Michelson, you know, sees to it that I don't do too much, but let me tell you, it's hard to take it easy with the mess Roger's left me with." Marion motioned toward the house. "Don't say a word, but you wouldn't believe the trouble he dug us into. Foreclosure notices on the house, his car's been repoed. I hate to say it, but it's almost worse than his death. His life insurance policy and selling the boat should cover some of it, but I'm hoping the bank will work with me on the rest."

So, that's why they were selling the boat. Something still didn't add up though. If Roger was headed to the poor house, how did he still afford the lavish gifts he poured on Ann Marie? Was he just living above his means and it got out of hand? No way was I bringing that question up to Marion. She'd suffered enough because of Roger. That didn't mean I couldn't ask Eric about it. Maybe Roger had hidden funds somewhere that now belonged to Marion, like an off-shore bank account. The rich always seemed to have one of those; and if Roger did, Marion's financial situation wouldn't be so dire.

"I'm sorry. If there's anything I can do, or even if you just need someone to talk to, I'm here," I said.

"Thanks for that. I appreciate it." Marion switched gears. "As much as I'd like to sit here and chat though, I really don't have time. I have some paperwork to get over to the bank and fax into the insurance company before they close for the day." Marion seemed to be charged back up to full power. "Oh, and I have to stop by the florist. I keep forgetting to do that."

"Of course. I'll let you get to it. And if you think of anything I can help you with, let me know."

"Thanks, but I think we've got everything covered," she replied.

"Okay, well, I'll talk to you later then."

As we said our goodbyes, I'd already made up my mind that my next stop was to talk to Eric. Generally, I liked to wait a day or two before calling a guy after a date, but this was different and much bigger than dating protocol. Besides, I was pretty sure dating etiquette didn't apply to murder investigations. I was convinced Eric would know more about Roger's financial mess than anyone. I was also sure he could keep a secret. After all, people trusted him with their financial futures every day. That had to count for something.

ERIC WAS KNEELING on the floor under the reception desk when I walked in. His black leather loafers stuck out at the end like a little kid who wasn't very good at hiding. He was mumbling to himself and dropped a swear word or two that came out louder than he probably expected. I laughed to myself. He looked slightly ridiculous and I couldn't help but smile, wondering what in the world he was up to.

"Hello?" I rapped on the door with my knuckle.

Eric jumped.

"Sorry, I didn't mean to startle you," I said, half laughing. Eric stood and straightened his jacket. The surprise on his face was quickly replaced with a smile. He looked anything but flustered in his black pinstriped suit. He had skipped the tie once again and left the top button open, giving off that sexy businessman look he was so good at. I started wondering what his closet must look like. It was definitely a walk-in, probably organized to a "T" with rows of tailored suits, silk ties, shined shoes, and leather belts. I pictured it right down to the impressive square footage and wooden hangers. I doubted the man owned a pair of jeans. Khakis were probably as low brow as he went. Yep, I was definitely more attracted to the guy's style than his clothes, if I was sitting here imagining his closet.

"Sorry I keep stopping by," I said, not meeting his eyes.

"Oh, no. It's fine. It's just, these files...," Eric pointed down to the floor. "They're a complete mess." I peeked over the desk and witnessed the disarray for myself.

"Where's your secretary?" Filing had to be part of her job description. I was surprised she hadn't taken to the task with the same fervor she had acting as gatekeeper. Organization seemed right up her alley.

"Alicia's no longer employed here. There were a couple of, let's say, indiscretions that couldn't be ignored," he replied. *Like the fact that she was a total witch*, I thought. I wonder what Tart did to finally get the heave ho. Truthfully, I couldn't fathom how she ever got hired in the first place.

Wait, who was I kidding? From the type of guy I'd learned Roger was, I'm sure Alicia hadn't been hired for her friendly disposition or typing skills.

"Sorry to hear that," I lied.

"No, you're not." Eric smiled. It was funny how quickly he read me. "And that's okay, because I wasn't either. She was terrible at the job and would've been let go a long time ago if Roger had allowed it."

"My friend Aria used to temp before she got married. I could see if she could help you out for a bit." Personally, I knew Aria hated temping, but I figured she'd be willing to do me a favor, especially knowing that it was a short-term gig, and she wouldn't get roped into anything more.

"That'd be great. I have a call into a staffing agency, but I think I'm going to be a little more selective with perspective hires this time."

I peeked over the desk again. He may have been a hell of a businessman, but when it came to filing, Eric didn't have a clue as to what he was doing. "It might only be for a couple hours a week, but I'll have her give you a call as soon as she can."

"Anything would be great. Thank you." The look on Eric's face was a little too sincere. I had to break eye contact before he made a move, and I found myself in an awkward situation. I knew how I felt about Eric, but it looked like he still considered me dating material.

Eric picked up on my body language and backed up. "Here, just give me a minute to gather these together and then we can talk."

"Sure, no problem." I walked around the lobby and scanned the business magazines, while Eric disappeared back under the desk. It only took a minute and he was ready to join me. We both sat down on the lobby's chairs.

"You know, I never could understand Roger's filing system. You think it would've killed him to use a computer."

"Nice." *Talk about the wrong thing to say.*

"Sorry, bad choice of words. I'm just frustrated. This is just such a mess."

I knew he was talking about more than just the files. "I know what you mean. It's gotta start getting better though, right?" That's me, the forever optimist.

"I hope you're right."

I hoped I was too.

"Anyway, enough about my problems. What can I do for you?" he asked.

"I know this isn't the best time, but there's something I want to talk to you about. It's a private matter and really not my business, but I have to ask."

Eric adopted a solemn expression. "What, what is it?"

"How was Roger doing? Financially I mean. Is the company going bankrupt?" I hadn't planned on blurting the question out like that. It just came out that way.

Eric was dumbfounded for a moment. "Bankrupt? Why would you think that?"

I tried to come up with a more tactful explanation.

"I had a talk with Marion this morning, and she said something about having financial difficulties." That was probably the nicest way to put what she had said. "Don't say anything to her, but I wanted to get your take on it. After all, if that is the case, maybe there's something linking Roger's finances to the murders."

Eric appeared to think the situation through before replying, "Well, Roger handled the company finances, but he never gave any indication of the sort. Frankly, I'd have a hard time believing it."

I thought so too, not only because of Roger's gifts to Ann Marie, but also judging by Eric's expensive wardrobe. It didn't appear SIS had a hard time making payroll.

"So, why do you think Roger wasn't paying the mortgage?" I asked.

"Are you sure that's what Marion said?"

"Positive. She's really stressed about it."

"I doubt Roger was really strapped for cash. Knowing him, he only wanted Marion to think he was."

Well, wasn't that just rotten.

"Why would he do that?" I didn't think it was possible

for my impression of Roger to get any lower, yet it was sinking further by the minute. Roger rated about one level below sludge.

"I can only guess, but knowing Roger, it had something to do with the state of his marriage."

I gave him a funny look. I wasn't following.

"Marion wouldn't be able to demand more alimony if she didn't think Roger had the money," Eric explained.

If you asked me, it was official—Roger was a horrible person. The worst of mankind. Any hope I had of any redeeming qualities vanished. I'm thinking karma may have had a larger role in his demise than I previously thought. I'd reached the point that, if I hadn't been attacked or threatened, I might not be so zealous to track down the murderer.

"I'll look into it though. Maybe I'm mistaken. I hope to hell I'm not," he said.

I didn't blame him. First, his business partner is murdered, then he finds out his business might be tanking? *Well, aren't I just the happy fairy.* It's a shame I left my glitter and unicorn at home.

"I have a favor to ask. Keep this business between you and me. I don't need is for the press to get wind of this," Eric said.

"Of course. And don't let Marion know I told you, got it?" The last thing I needed was for my clients thinking I was gossiping about them. Clients' secrets weren't mine to tell, but sometimes they were so hard to keep.

"Agreed." Eric's eyes got that googly look again. *I think we just shared a moment.* I checked my inner-radar again. Nope, he still wasn't dating material.

"What are you doing this Saturday? Do you have any plans?" he asked.

I tried to think quickly. I always hated this part. Letting a guy down was awkward, no matter how you worded it. Eric must have sensed what was coming because he quickly changed tactics.

"It's just, I promised you I'd help digitize those files. I was thinking this Saturday would be a good time to do that," he said.

"Oh, yeah, for sure." That was something I could agree to. It would also give me time to think of a way to put Eric firmly in the friend category.

12

*I*t felt good to be home. I flicked on the television and settled on the couch with a warm fuzzy blanket and a big bowl of mint chocolate chip ice cream. Today, I felt like I had earned some lazy *me* time.

I hadn't flipped through all the channels, when a muffled ring came from my purse on the table. *Seriously?* I assumed it was Mrs. J. Patsy Ann probably told her all about the note on my car, and Mrs. J. was eager for the details. Right now, I didn't care what she wanted. She could just wait.

When the second call came in, less than a minute later, I started second guessing myself. For once, Detective Brandle might be calling, or maybe it was Finn. Not that I wanted him to call. Wait, did I want him to call? Ugh, men were so confusing. This is why I had been avoiding relationships. Truth be told, I wouldn't be able to move on with anyone until I had closure with Finn, or at least some answers. That wasn't asking for too much. That last thought was enough to make me run over to my phone and to try and catch it before the call went to voicemail. I wasn't quick enough.

While I waited to see if the caller would leave a message, I scrolled through the phone's call log. I didn't recognize the last two numbers. One of them had left a message. My voicemail chimed soon after.

I dialed into my mailbox and waited for the voice to instruct me to enter my security code. Per the recording, I had two new messages. I was right about the first one. It was Mrs. J. She claimed she was calling to set up a makeover party for her granddaughter Georgia's sixteenth birthday. I hadn't done one of those before but was open to the idea. The second message, and the one that I was most eager to hear, was from Philip Siebold. He said his mom had told him about me and what had happened at their house. He was wondering if we could meet up tonight to talk. I pulled the phone away from my ear and looked at the time. It seemed much later than seven o'clock. Not that the time mattered. I would've agreed to meet him even if it was midnight.

I went into the missed-calls log on my phone, found the second unfamiliar number, and hit *send*. The phone rang five times. I thought that it was going to go to voicemail when Philip picked up.

"Philip Siebold."

"Hi, Philip, its Ziva Diaz."

He paused before speaking. I wasn't sure if it was because he didn't recollect my name, or if he was surprised that I had returned his call so quickly. My guess was the later.

"Hi, Ziva. Thanks for getting back with me," he said.

"Yeah, no problem. What's up?"

"I've been trying to piece together what happened. It sounds like you're the person I need to talk to. Any way you'd be willing to meet up?" Philip sounded all business. I respected that. He seemed just as eager to solve this case as I was. *Then again, he could really be the murderer and just be trying to figure out how much I know.* I'd have to tread lightly.

"I could do that. Do you know where Sweet Thangs is?" I asked.

"Is it still off North Bay Street?" Philip asked.

"It is."

"Okay. I can meet you there. Say, in about an hour?"

"That works. I'll see you soon then." As I hung up, I only had one question on my mind: what does one wear to interview a murder suspect?

I TORE THROUGH MY CLOSET, trying to come up with the perfect outfit. I thought about going with the red dress again. After all, red was a power color and I was planning on getting some answers. However, in the end, comfort won out. I went with a new pair of plum-colored leggings with a light-weight black sweater and tan suede ankle boots. The look was more cute than sexy and hopefully gave off an innocent, unintimidating vibe.

When I pulled up to Sweet Thangs, I noticed it was much quieter tonight. Only a handful of people were inside, and that included the workers. Philip's silver BMW was parked out front, so I knew he was already there. A quick scan of the patrons told me he was most likely the hand-some-looking man, wearing a light-yellow polo shirt, sitting at a back table. His head was down, reading something on his phone, but I was fairly certain it was him.

I walked toward the table, taking a moment to glance up along the way at the daily drink specials written in pink chalk on the blackboard. I don't know why I bothered. I ordered the same drink every time, but maybe tonight I would get some dessert to go, seeing how I had a half bowl of melted chocolate chip ice cream sitting on the counter at home.

"Philip?" I asked when I reached the table.

"Ziva, thank you so much for meeting me. Sorry, work." He motioned to his phone before standing to shake my hand. Up close, Philip's resemblance to Roger was unmistakable. They had the same smile and slate-gray eyes.

"I meant to call you earlier, but it's been nonstop since I got into town," he said.

I pulled back the white H-shaped chair, and sat down. "I can imagine. I've been pretty busy myself."

"That's right. Mom said you own your own business?" he asked.

"Yeah, I'm a consultant for Beauty Secrets, the skin care and makeup company."

"I see how you two know each other then," Philip said with a genuine smile. Contrary to what Mrs. J. thought, I was betting Marion's love for lipstick started long before she got sick.

"You got it. Your mom's one of my top clients." It was selfish of me to think where my profit margin would be without Marion's business, yet I was thinking about it. Looked like Eric was rubbing off on me more than I realized.

"But, I still don't understand why you were in the house if she wasn't home." Philip seemed genuinely confused.

"That's easy. I was making a delivery. Like most of my clients, your mom and I have a designated drop off spot in case I stop by while she's out, which was the case on Saturday."

The barista stopped by to take our drink orders. I, of

course, went with the chai latte. Philip went with a cappuccino.

"How's your mom doing by the way?" I asked when it was just us again. I thought it'd be interesting to get Philip's take on Marion's behavior.

"Surprisingly well. I don't know if she's in denial or what, but she seems to be doing well. I understand you're partially to thank for that."

"I'm not sure about that. I think Dr. Michelson and Eric have been a bigger help then I have." I was hoping to lead the conversation toward Dr. Michelson, but Philip went off in an entirely different direction.

"Ah, good old Eric, my father's little lap dog. How I hate that man." The angered expression on his face told me he was sincere in his disdain. He stared down the napkin dispenser on the table, and I would've paid big money to know what he was thinking.

I waited for him to elaborate. When he didn't, I said, "Hang on, you can't just say something like that and not explain yourself." Especially seeing that I was meeting up with the guy again on Saturday and contemplating a business venture with him. If he's a dog, I'd like to find that out sooner rather than later.

"Okay, I take that back. Technically, it's not Eric's fault he's the son my father always wanted, but the way he idolized the man drove me nuts. Like my father could do no wrong."

Ah, now we were getting somewhere.

"And your father could do plenty wrong?" Playing the naive card seemed like the right way to go. I wondered what version of Roger, Philip would introduce me to.

Philip leaned back to read me for a minute. I'm not sure what he saw, but he quickly made up his mind.

Looked like I had gone with the right outfit. Innocent for the win!

"What do you know about Delgado Enterprises?" Philip asked me.

"Who?" I wasn't following the conversation. I thought for sure he was going to bring up Ann Marie or maybe another one of his father's former mistresses. Philip could've easily asked me about astrophysics and gotten the same look. I mouthed the name and looked up at the ceiling tiles for the answer. I was coming up blank.

"They're a shipping brokerage firm," he supplied. The name still didn't register. Leaning across the table, he added, "The Port of Savannah is the fastest growing seaport in the U.S. Big money comes in through these waters, and not all of it's clean. It's rumored that Delgado Enterprises will ship and insure any goods out of the U.S. for a price."

Philip leaned back and the barista placed our drinks on the table. We both thanked her, but left the drinks untouched.

"And what does that mean?" I asked.

"It means, my father didn't care where the money came from as long as he could get rich off investing it. Vincent Delgado approached my father a couple of years ago, about a business deal. It was around the same time I was set to join his firm."

"You're an investment banker?"

"Bond trader." There was a difference? I nodded like I understood anyway. "The plan had been for me to join SIS after spending a few years navigating the New York market. I didn't care to work for him, but I knew how much it meant to my mom, so I thought I'd give it a go."

"That's commendable," I said as I picked up my drink. I could only ignore perfection for so long.

"Well it was, until my father approached me about representing Delgado. The crook had a reputation, even in New York, and I knew what his money meant."

"So, what did you do?" I asked.

"I flat out refused and couldn't believe my father was greedy enough to take his money. I said some things that needed to be said and, after that, decided to stay in New York. If my father wanted to choose Delgado's money over me, then to hell with him."

"Amen," I said and took another sip of my drink.

We both fell silent, lost in our own respective thoughts. I was thinking that I could absolutely see where Philip was coming from, where his dad was concerned. If I were him, I wouldn't care much for Roger either. Unfortunately for Marion, that meant missing out on time with her son, which was heartbreaking. The whole situation sucked. I think the worst part was that it wouldn't have had to be that way if Roger hadn't been so greedy.

"Eric never mentioned any of this to you?" Philip finally asked.

"Not a word. Then again, why would he?" I asked.

"Because investing for Delgado is like working for the mafia. Eric knows that. If he really wanted to help solve the case, he would've told the police to look there first." Philip leaned back and he look convinced that Delgado was his man, or rather someone that worked for him.

Surrounded by coffee and cupcakes, I realized how deep this case could go. I would have to be careful moving forward. Cement shoes were not my style. I was not about to go swimming with the fishies.

"Do you know the detective working the case?" Philip asked.

"Detective Brandle? Yeah. I don't know him really well, but I've talked to him a time or two."

"Is there some secret to getting in touch with him, because he hasn't returned a single one of my calls," Philip said.

"Ah, good luck with that. It's definitely hit or miss with him. The man's overworked, to say the least." I was hoping Detective Brandle was devoting more time to the case, but Philip's comment made me skeptical.

"I heard you were there when they found the girlfriend's body," Philip said.

I thought carefully before responding, not sure where this conversation was going.

"I was," I said.

"How did they find her?" he asked.

"You mean, what did she look like?" Well there was a morbid question. I was not about to go there. Not only that, but it creeped me out just thinking about it.

"No, no. I mean why were they searching the boat? Hadn't the police already done that?"

"Your mom knows the answer to that one. They were prepping the boat for potential buyers. A walk-through was scheduled that morning," I said.

"I hadn't heard," he replied.

"Oh. Well, a friend of mine was dropping some paperwork off on board, and I was just tagging along when we found her." *It just happened to be really bad luck on my part*, I thought to myself.

Philip grew silent and stared out the window, drinking his cappuccino. The glittering rays of the sun had finally set. Outside, streetlamps buzzed as their bulbs flickered on. The light inside Sweet Thangs appeared to brighten. For the first time, I noticed Philip was wearing a silver wedding band. I pointed to the ring and asked, "Did you come here alone? Marion didn't mention anything about your wife."

Philip laughed like I was missing something. "Yeah, I came down a few days early. My husband, Scott, is flying in tomorrow."

"Ah, gotcha. Sorry for assuming." Heat rose to my face and I was embarrassed, to say the least. Glad I skipped the red dress. Female persuasion wouldn't have gotten me very far.

"No, that's okay. It was just another part of my life my father didn't approve of." Philip's face adopted a scowl again.

"You two never got along, did you?" It was more of a statement than a question.

"No. Never." I couldn't tell if Philip was more angered or annoyed at his father's lack of acceptance. I had a feeling that even if Roger had lived to be a hundred, that would've never changed.

I DIDN'T HAVE to be embarrassed for long. Shortly after the husband comment, Philip announced that he should be going. He thanked me for meeting with him and then offered to walk me out. I waited until he pulled away in his car before jumping in my pickup to head home. Only, I didn't feel like going straight home. Instead, I drove around aimlessly, zigzagging through neighborhoods, heading past the elementary school, and eventually driving along the coast. I didn't know where I was going, until I pulled in the marina and found myself staring up at Finn's apartment. *Ugh, stupid boys.* I wondered if Ms. Mystery woman was up there right now. The thought made my stomach churn.

My phone rang in my purse. I quickly retrieved it and

looked at the caller ID. It was Finn! *You've got to be kidding me.* My stomach churned again. I looked around. Could he see me right now? Sweet sugar, how embarrassing. There was no point in not answering it, if he could. I'd just have to come up with a story quick enough, like leaving something at his place last night. Yeah, that sounded good. I was going with that.

Reluctantly, I answered the phone. "Hello?"

"Hey, Ziva, how's it going?"

"It's going all right. How about yourself?" I tried to hide the reluctance in my voice and let Finn steer the conversation.

"Not too bad. I'm just driving back home and thought I'd give you a call, seeing how I didn't get to say goodbye yesterday morning." I couldn't get any luckier. *My nan must be working overtime.* I started the pickup and backed out, trying to get out of there before Finn made it back home.

"Oh, well, thanks. I'm doing good though." I didn't want to dwell on Finn's sweet gesture. It looked like I was on his mind as much as he was on mine. Not that it mattered. He could think about me all day, but it wouldn't change the fact that he had a girlfriend. I got my thoughts back on track and pulled out of the marina to start driving home.

"Hey, guess who I just talked to?" I said, putting an end to that conversation.

"Who?" he asked.

"Philip Siebold. You know, Marion and Roger's son?" I replied.

"As in, the man you think might have attacked you and murdered his father?" Finn couldn't have sounded more incredulous.

"That's beside the point. I don't think that anymore.

Well, I guess he could still be a suspect, but that's not the point," I said.

"No, that *is* the point," Finn said, not backing down.

"No, no, no. Just listen. According to Philip, Roger was involved in some shady business practices. Have you heard of a man named Vincent Delgado?" I asked.

"Dang, Ziva, you're killing me. That's bad. If Delgado's involved, I don't want to hear another word." Yep, Finn was good and ticked off now. It was clear that he didn't see this turn of events as a positive development.

I tried to play it down a bit. "Well, I don't know if he is exactly," I said.

"What do you mean? What did Philip say?" Finn asked.

"I thought you didn't want to hear another word?" Yep, that's me. Ziva Diaz, smart ass, at your service.

"Come on now," Finn said. Was that exasperation I heard? Surely, that must be a better emotion than anger? That's what I was hoping anyway.

"Okay, okay. What he said exactly was that his father was investing Delgado's money, and that if he were the police, he'd look there first. He said he was surprised I didn't know anything about it."

"Why would you?" he asked.

"I know, right? That's what I said." I was glad Finn was following my train of thought. "Philip thinks Eric should have said something. I know he didn't say anything to me, but I have no idea if he said something to Detective Brandle." I really needed to talk to the detective and find out.

"Do you think Eric told him?" Finn asked.

"I have no idea. I'm going to try and call Detective Brandle next."

"Good idea. Just be careful. God only knows how far up this case goes. Maybe it's time you backed out of it." That reminded me, I hadn't said anything to Finn about the note on my car.

"There hasn't been anyone suspicious hanging out by the docks, has there?" I asked.

"Not that I can think of. Why? What's going on?" Finn sounded back on edge again.

"A note was left on my car the night I stayed at your place. Someone telling me to back off or else. Let me know if you see anyone or if someone says anything."

Finn gave an honest to goodness sigh. "I haven't heard anything, but I can ask around. Did you call the cops?" he asked.

"Yeah, Detective Brandle met me right away. He couldn't do much but collect some evidence. Not sure if anything will come of it."

"Are you okay?" Finn seemed to be asking me that a lot lately. I wanted to tell him that I was fine; but at that moment, I couldn't. I had just parked the truck in front of my apartment and was gathering my things, when I froze. Something wasn't right. I got the feeling someone was watching me yet again, but I couldn't spot them. I was getting mighty sick of that feeling.

The parking lot was deserted. The antique shop had closed hours before. No one was on the street either. I looked up to my apartment and saw that inside was pitch black. Not a single light was on, and I knew that wasn't right. I had left the living room lamp on, and the outside light, before meeting Philip.

I grabbed the pepper spray on my key chain and looked around me, ready for a fight. No one jumped out at me, but that didn't mean no one was there. The rational part of my brain insisted that a fuse inside was just blown. It wouldn't be the first time I'd come home with no power; but tonight, I had a feeling the wiring wasn't to blame for the darkness upstairs.

"Ziva? Ziva, you there?" Finn asked.

"Yeah, hold on a sec." I wanted to keep Finn on the line in case I needed him to call the cops, but I couldn't really talk to him right then. I needed to focus on my surroundings. Real quiet-like, I made my way up my outside staircase, scanning the area with every step. If someone was inside my apartment, I was ready to greet whoever with a can of pepper spray to the face.

At the top of the stairs, the front door to my apartment had been jimmied. The lock no longer clicked shut, from the abuse. I nudged the door open with my foot, keeping my shoulder against the building, ready for someone to attack. At that moment, I would've preferred a fight to the heavy silence that pressed on my chest. Hearing nothing, I peeked my head around and looked inside the door. *Oh sweet, sweet sugar.* In the dark, I could start to make out the mess. Someone had paid me a visit and left a wake of destruction in their path.

"Finn, I need to call you back. Someone just broke into my place." I didn't even wait to hear what he said. I had already hung up and dialed 9-1-1.

he Detective had kept his word about the added patrols in my neighborhood, but it hadn't done me any good. Within a few minutes, the two uniformed officers assigned to my area were at my apartment, ready to secure the scene. I waited for them in my car, not wanting to touch anything inside until they scoped things out. Finn came racing over right after them, no doubt ignoring all posted speed limits. I was happy, despite myself, to see him. By the time Detective Brandle joined us, we were a happy little party.

The police department didn't have the resources to go all CSI on the place, but after ensuring the perpetrator was gone and dusting the door knob for prints, they let me survey the damage. My couch was turned over, with every cushion thrown about. The stuffing was even slashed out of one of them. I appreciated that my throw pillows were still intact, but they were about the only items that was spared. The kitchen was a disaster. Food and dishes had been dumped out of the cupboards all over the countertops. A vase filled with white roses was shattered on the floor. Water and glass glittered off the hardwood. At my desk, client records were thrown about, pages torn directly from my *Beauty Bible* and ripped in pieces. It was a disaster. My computer screen was sliced from corner to corner, and the glass desk it sat on had been cracked by something heavy, like a hammer. In my bedroom, it looked like my whole closet had been dumped out—shoes, clothes, and handbags thrown everywhere. And of course, my jewelry box had been ransacked.

I sifted through my jewelry box to see what was missing, only to find that the bastard had stolen my engagement ring. Not that I cared about the ring itself, but it was my financial safety net. Just one night before, I was thinking of selling the ring and using the cash to fund my new beauty business. Dinner with Eric had left me inspired. The three-carat canary diamond was spectacular, and was sure to bring a hefty price tag. Unfortunately, when it came to my past relationship, more money didn't equate to more love. No way was my ex getting that beauty back, but now it was in the hands of someone else, who was sure to make a small fortune off it. I chastised myself for not keeping it someplace safer. Then again, I never thought someone would rob me. I guess you could say, lesson learned. A painful, gut-wrenching lesson.

Finn, who had kept silent up until that point, stepped back and asked, "What? What is it?"

"Nothing." I slammed my jewelry box lid shut. I didn't feel like talking about ex-fiancés with Finn at the moment.

In the bathroom, I stopped short. My entire makeup collection, and we're talking drawers and drawers of lipstick, mascara, and eye shadow; had been smashed and dumped everywhere. Powders and creams stained the white soapstone countertops and bathroom rugs. Above the mess, scrawled on the bathroom mirror in red lipstick, were the words "NEXT TIME" with the picture of a smiley face with a bullet in the head. Of course, he had to ruin my favorite lipstick in the process.

"Oh, you're right about next time," I said. "Next time, you'd better pray I'm not home."

I walked out to the kitchen. Detective Brandle and Finn were motionless behind me. With one swoop of my arm, I cleared off the kitchen counter. Corn flakes and chocolate candies rained down into the sink. Without a word, I got out a martini glass from the cabinet above the refrigerator and made myself a gin martini, taking a swig off the gin bottle before picking up the vermouth to add a splash to my glass. I offered the gin bottle to the gentlemen, but they both declined. Finn kept looking at me like I'd lost my mind. It was obvious he'd never seen me pissed off before.

I assessed the damage in my head. Next to the ring, it didn't look like anything had been stolen. This was more of a seek-and-destroy mission—a way to get under my skin— or, rather, an attempt to try and scare me straight. I was betting a man was behind the break in, too, because no way could a woman rummage through my closet and not swipe at least one pair of heels or a handbag. Everyone knew what a diamond was worth, but designers were harder to price. I immediately thought of Delgado. If he really ran his business like the mafia, then this type of stunt seemed right up his alley. After all, the mafia never went after just the person. They played mind games—hurting your family, your business, and your livelihood before hurting you.

I took that minute to relay what Philip had told me about Roger and Delgado, to Detective Brandle.

"And he knows for certain Roger worked for Delgado?" Detective Brandle asked.

"He seemed certain of it to me," I said.

"Excuse me." The name Delgado sparked something within the detective. He was talking rapidly on his phone before he even made it out my front door. He looked like he hit pay dirt.

"Why don't you stay at my place tonight and we can start cleaning up here in the morning?" Finn offered.

Fat chance of that, I thought. One, I wouldn't be able to sleep tonight, knowing the mess that awaited me; and two, I didn't want to deal with Finn's girlfriend - or whatever she was - banging on the door at seven AM. "I'm too keyed up to sleep. I'd rather tackle this now than wait until morning." I swirled my martini and took a drink.

Finn went to stay something but caught my eye. He must've seen something to make him change his mind. I was in no mood to argue. "Okay, if you're sure, I'll go and get supplies to fix your door. You can't stay here without a front door that locks," he said.

I downed the rest of my drink while he talked. "Good thinking," I said. "And pick up some more gin while you're at it, and maybe some chocolates." Who knew how long this night was going to last?

Detective Brandle stood outside, talking on his phone while Finn was gone. I ignored his conversation and tackled the mess instead. It was amazing how productive you could be with a martini in one hand and a trash bag in the other. I didn't even bother sorting the dishes. If they were chipped, they got tossed. I threw out all the food from the open cupboards too. I just couldn't trust it. I worked in a flurry because I knew that if I even stopped for just a minute, I'd either have a breakdown, or end up breaking something. Neither option would help me put my apartment back in order.

As I moved on to the bathroom, I couldn't help but feel grateful that I was a Beauty Secrets consultant; otherwise, it would've cost me a fortune to replace all the makeup. I shoveled the broken powdery shadows and smashed lipsticks into the trash with a dust pan. Turns out, that was the easy part. Getting the twelve-hour lipstick stain off the bathroom mirror was the challenge. Part of me was proud that my product lived up to its claim. The other part was deeply annoyed at the smudged letters that refused to budge. As a last-ditch effort, I dipped a wash rag into my martini glass and gave that a go. Turns out, alcohol did the trick. The lipstick stain disappeared and left me with a streak-free shine. I started to think that I should clean with a martini more often.

Finn came back as I was righting the couch and fluffing the remaining throw pillows. I couldn't bring myself to tackle my bedroom. That task required mental clarity, which I currently lacked. "Here, I wasn't sure which one you wanted." Finn tossed me a bag of chocolate-covered pretzels, and put a couple of candy bars next to a new bottle of gin on the kitchen table. He bought the expensive kind too. Tonight, it was top shelf all the way.

"Thanks." I tore open the bag of pretzels and munched happily away on the sweet-and-salty snack. It was the perfect complement to my cocktail.

Finn strapped on a tool belt and got to work fixing my door. I tried to ignore how hot he looked in his contractor get up, but it was hard. It must have been the liquor kicking in. To keep my mind busy, I started gathering client papers and tried to make sense of my *Beauty Bible*. First thing tomorrow, I was calling my insurance agent and then buying a new computer. It was time for me to digitalize my files and back them up online somewhere. I was glad I had made plans with Eric to tackle the first step on Saturday.

"Detective Brandle left?" I'd just noticed the detective was no longer outside the door.

"Yeah, he left when I got back." Finn had busted out the big guns and was now drilling a hole above the new lock he had installed. "Deadbolt," he added when he saw my expression. Good thing he couldn't read my thoughts because I was actually thinking, *You can bring power tools over to my place anytime.*

I took a break from taping and alphabetizing my invoices, and stood up to survey the room. It wasn't perfect, but it was better. "Can I get you anything?" I shouted over the drilling.

Finn pointed to a large fountain pop on the counter. I shouldn't have been surprised. He did have a thing for cola. I went to the kitchen anyway and rummaged in the freezer. Apparently, the burglar didn't feel the need to trash my tater-tot stash. I threw a layer of the frozen fried potatoes onto a cookie sheet and put them in the oven. I thought about making another martini while I waited, but I'd already had one too many. I filled a glass up with water from the tap instead.

"That should do it." Finn double checked that the deadbolt and lock were properly working. "Are you sure you don't want to stay at my place, or I could stay here?" And here was the problem with answering Finn's question. I wanted him to stay, but I shouldn't have. I should've still been pissed about the girl-at-the-door incident, and demanded answers, or at least asked the guy about her. I didn't feel like being responsible though. My mind was full of all sorts of dirty thoughts. *We could do it on the couch, the bed, the kitchen table... heck, I'd take him on the living room floor, given the chance. Gah!*

Finn had to leave, and maybe take the gin with him. No way could I keep my hands off him if he spent the night, which is exactly why he couldn't stay. Well, not until I sorted out the whole mystery-woman thing, and that wasn't a conversation I felt like having tonight, for a few reasons. One: if she did turn out to be his girlfriend, that would just be too crushing. And, two: if she wasn't, well, I didn't want to be drunk the first time Finn and I hooked up. Then there was the whole Eric situation. I knew I didn't like him like that, but he didn't know it. It didn't feel right moving on with someone else until Eric knew where we stood. I tell you, my love life was like feast or famine.

Finn was probably thinking I was mental because it took way too long for me to respond with, "I'm good."

Gah again! Did that sound as pathetic I think it did? I tried not to sigh, but I wasn't very successful. I shook my head to clear it, and attempted to elaborate, "I mean, thanks for the offer, and for fixing my door. I doubt whoever did this is going to come back tonight though. I imagine they think I'd be too scared to hang around," I said.

"Then that person's an idiot," Finn replied, with a slight smile.

Aw, crap. What a sweet thing to say. Finn really had to go before one of us made a move, and I wouldn't be able to say no.

"Listen, I'm going to eat my tater tots and go to bed. I'll call you tomorrow or something, and maybe we can hang out." *And I can finally ask you about the mystery woman.*

Finn looked just as disappointed as I felt, but he managed to say, "Sure, that sounds good." I felt bad, but that was the best offer he was going to get. "Call me if you need anything. I'll be up for a while," he said on his way out.

"Thanks, I will." I locked the deadbolt behind him, and stood at the door for a minute, feeling conflicted. I didn't want him to leave, but I knew I made the right decision. Being a responsible adult sucked.

It was a good thing I had a whole cookie sheet of tater tots to eat, because it was going to be a long time before I'd be able to settle down and think about anything other than Finn and that damn tool belt.

"SWEET SUGAR," I mumbled in my sleep. "Leave me alone." I had fallen asleep on the couch that night, not wanting to mess with my room, with my cell phone a little too close by. The annoying ringtone echoed in my ear. I swatted the phone onto the floor. It clattered on the hardwood and woke me up the rest of the way. Lord help me, if it was Mrs. J....

It wasn't. It was Eric. "Ziva, you were right," he said when I answered.

"Right about what?" I asked.

"Roger. I stayed up all night piecing together his files. He was bankrupt, or headed that way, until he started padding his accounts."

"What do you mean?" I wasn't awake enough for this conversation. What time was it anyway? My head was screaming for ibuprofen.

"Roger was stealing from his clients. Well, actually, just one—Vincent Delgado," Eric said.

"Wow, wait, what? He was stealing from Delgado?" I wanted to make sure I understood what Eric was saying. I'd definitely be nursing a hangover today.

"You got it," he said with excitement in his voice.

"That's crazy. Why would he do that?" I asked.

"I know it is. I don't understand it either. Maybe Detective Brandle can figure it all out. I wanted to call you first though, and thank you for the tip. I would've never considered Roger's personal finances if you hadn't said something."

"But you knew Roger worked for Delgado," I said.

"I did, and I know what you're thinking. I should've told the police first; but honestly, I forgot about it. Delgado Enterprises was a private contract between Roger and Vincent. I had nothing to do with it. Poor excuse, I know, but it's the truth."

"Well, his reputation sure fits the bill, and it seems like he had more than enough motivation if Roger was stealing from him. Maybe it really is all that simple." Even as I said the words, I didn't quite believe them. Something was off, but I couldn't figure out what. Maybe after I got rid of my headache and ate some breakfast, I'd be able to make better sense of it.

"Listen, I'm going to call Detective Brandle right now, but are we still on for tomorrow night?" Eric asked.

Tomorrow night. Digitizing my *Beauty Bible.* That's right. I so wasn't feeling it, but knew it needed to get done. Besides, it's not like it was a second date. Just a business meeting. I could even draft up my business plan before then and give it to him to review.

"Yeah, I'll be there. Seven o'clock?" I asked.

"That's what I was thinking, unless a different time works better for you."

"No, seven's fine. I'll see you then." I hung up with Eric and took inventory of my apartment in the daylight. It didn't look too bad, until I entered my bedroom. I had a lot of work to do. I found myself wondering where the chocolate was again, because this was going to take a while.

The rest of my morning was spent on the phone with my insurance agent, and in my room making sense of the chaos. I took a mid-morning break and ran down a couple store-fronts to the diner for the hungry-man special where I devoured steak, eggs, home fries, Texas toast, and a choco-late shake in record time. My hangover was feeling better by the minute, and I didn't even take the time to guilt myself over my poor eating habits. Win-win.

Back at my apartment, I kept thinking my engagement ring was tossed somewhere in the mess; but nope, that baby was gone. My insurance agent was checking to see what my jewelry coverage was. I doubted it was enough. In the mean-time, I needed to go out and purchase a new computer, a desk, and some fancy dinnerware to replace the dishes I tossed the night before. By two o'clock that afternoon, I was done, both mentally and physically. My apartment, the bedroom included, resembled some sense of normalcy, and I felt a bit of order had been restored. Now it was time to do some shopping.

I got into my truck and was about to head to the big box electronics store to replace my computer, when I remem-bered I had to stop by my parents' condo and take the trash out before they got home. I forgot to set it out last week, and I knew their garage would be stinking up to the high heavens by now. That's what they get for keeping their trash cans in a warm, stuffy garage. If I had thought about it, I would've grabbed a can of air freshener on my way over. Maybe Mom still had some under the kitchen sink because, Lord knows, if they came home to a rotten-smelling garage, I'd never hear the end of it.

Typically, I was a responsible person; but I had to admit,

this week, I was dropping the ball. My diet sucked, I wasn't making any follow-up beauty calls, and all my parents' plants were probably dead. Not that I didn't have a lot going on. This whole murder business was really messing with my life. I was hopeful Detective Brandle was working the new leads and would have the case solved before next weekend. I could go back to doing my regular beauty gig without being paranoid, I'd never have to mention a word of it to my parents, and just maybe Eric could help me develop a business plan for striking out on my own. I got goosebumps just thinking about it.

As I drove to my parents' place, bits of conversations, theories, and facts from the last twenty-four hours swirled in my head. I kept wondering why, out of all his clients, Roger would choose Delgado to steal from, when he knew the man's reputation. There had to have been a dozen or more easier targets for him to go after, people who probably didn't check their bottom lines as often as Delgado. And how would Delgado know anything about me? Even if he was the one who attacked me in the Siebold's kitchen, it wasn't like I had identification on me and, so far, my name was kept out of the press. How would he know my involvement in this case or even where I lived? The case still had too many holes for Delgado to fill.

I was so wrapped up in my thoughts that it took me three left-hand turns and one four-way stop to realize I was following the white Mercedes in front of me. I backed off the gas and tried to let the car get ahead. I hated when cars followed me all the way home or through a subdivision. It always creeped me out. Often, I'd forgo my original destination just to be safe.

My plan didn't work. We both got the next red light. I couldn't help but check out the driver. His style with the slicked-back hair and aviator sunglasses matched his ride to a "T". The man looked up in his rearview mirror and caught me staring. I glanced away and peered down the street to my right, pretending to look for something important. The light turned green and I hung back. My turn off was up ahead, just a couple of streets away. No need to gas it out of the gate.

Turned out, the Mercedes wasn't in a hurry either. As we approached my parents' complex, I made sure to turn my blinker on far in advance. I was surprised when the Mercedes did the same.

"Sorry," I said, even though the guy couldn't hear me. I wasn't trying to be a creeper, or maybe he didn't care. Maybe girls only worried about things like that.

The security guard, Miles, was outside, stretching by his post when we pulled in. Knowing Miles, the afternoon matinee was on commercial break. That was about the only time the elderly man stepped outside the little square booth. When the Mercedes drove up, Miles waved and walked closer, leaning into the car's rolled-down window. The two men seemed to know each other quite well, talking as they did, and ignoring the fact that I was idling behind them. I was patient, more or less, because I had to be, and still smiled when Miles waved me through next.

When I pulled through, the Mercedes was directly ahead, weaving the same pattern through the complex's twists and turns that I needed to take. You'd think the driver lived there, but there was no way he was close to fifty, which was the complex's minimum age requirement. I figured he must have been here visiting someone just as I was; only, I was curious as to who.

Before the Mercedes pulled down my parents' street, I had already decided to follow it. I mean, I had followed him this far, might as well figure out who he was visiting. The driver tapped the breaks just past my parents' condo and slowed, pulling into Inez's driveway. Not wanting to seem like a stalker, I turned into my parents' driveway at the last minute and reached above to the sun visor for their garage door opener. But, I didn't park inside the garage. Tomorrow, after all, was trash day. I took advantage of the situation and fed my curiosity by rolling out the green plastic trash bin from the garage and taking it to the curb. It smelled awful. I struggled, wheeling the heavy bin down the driveway, while holding my breath and trying to keep an eye on Inez's visitor.

The result was a disaster. I knew there was a crack at the bottom of the driveway; but of course, I wasn't thinking about it. As the bin's front set of wheels hit the crack, the whole bin wobbled sideways, popping the top off it, sending a stomach-churning wave of pungent trash odor up my nose. I almost tossed my cookies. The trash bags fell out into the driveway, and the empty bin skidded into the road. I created more of a scene than I had meant to, and quickly retrieved the trash bin and hefted a bag of trash back into it.

"Here, let me help you." Inez's visitor was picking up another trash bag in his designer suit coat and jeans before I could even say thank you. I was betting Eric and this guy knew each other, based upon the way they dressed.

I bent down to pick up the last trash bag and, when I stood back up and met the man's eyes, I was thrown back to the night at the strip club. What was the Boss Man doing at Inez's house? I was positive it was him. My mouth tingled like it did when I had a sugar rush, and I knew I was on to something.

"Thanks for your help—"

"Delgado, Vincent Delgado." The man filled in his name.

Holy hell. I wasn't prepared for that one. I took a step back like prey does when it realizes it's caught the attention of a predator.

Danger, danger, my mind signaled to me.

What the higgidy heck was Delgado doing here? Did he know where I was headed and he was trying to get me alone? I plastered on a megawatt smile and tried to form a coherent thought. I looked around to see if any neighbors were out. Mr. Willard was walking his toy poodle a half a block ahead, but he would be useless if Delgado made a move.

What I learned in that moment was that when faced with a dangerous situation, only two possibilities exist—fight or flight. I'm embarrassed to say that in this case I high-tailed it out of there as fast as my heels would take me. I thanked Delgado again for his help and marched straight up the driveway, through the garage, and up to the back door. I jiggled the door knob a few times before realizing that I never unlocked it. My keys were still in my truck. I walked along the side edge of the garage and peered out. Delgado was gone, but his car was still there. I dashed out to my truck, as if it were pouring rain, and grabbed my purse through the rolled-down window. Running back, I had the door unlocked, locked, and dead bolted in five seconds flat. The crazy smile stayed stuck on my face the entire time.

I crept around the condo as if Delgado were watching me, keeping a low profile and avoiding walking in front of open windows. In the hallway, I walked sideways with my back against the banister, pausing at the front door to peer out the peephole. I couldn't see anyone, but that didn't matter. My nerves were still charged with enough electricity to shock myself silly. *You followed **him***, I reminded myself. *Unless he knew where you were going,* my mind countered once more. I didn't see how that was possible, but I wasn't being the most rationale individual at the moment. Then, I struck on the most important question of all: what was Vincent Delgado doing at Inez's?

I tiptoed up the stairs, knowing the best vantage point was the guest bedroom window. Up in the room, I took position below the window frame and lifted one of the inch-thick horizontal blinds and looked out. Inez's place looked unremarkably quiet. I held my ground for a couple of minutes until my head became light. With a quick intake of air, I realized that I'd been holding my breath. "This is ridiculous." I dropped the blind and sat down, leaning against the wall. "I'm sure Delgado has a perfectly reasonable explanation for being at Inez's. This has nothing to do with you." See, I did still possess some common sense. The man probably thought I was a total nut ball for the way I just acted. I closed my eyes for a moment to regain my composure and center myself. All my yoga practice was coming in handy, and I was calm in no time.

The sound of a car door shutting, quickly changed that. I peered out the window so fast that I pitched myself forward and fell into the blinds. *So much for being inconspicuous.* My hand fumbled for the blind's dangling white cord, and I tugged it hard. The blinds shot up and swayed across the window from the force. It was too late. Delgado had disappeared.

"He's gone? Why? What's his hurry?" I was on my feet, down the stairs, and walking out the front door before I could reason with myself not to. I was just as bad as Mrs. J., running over to Inez's like this. What was I going to say when she opened the door? I should have grabbed a few beauty samples, or a catalog, something, anything to justify my visit.

I rang the bell anyway. Looked like I was going to have to pretend I was purely making a social call. Maybe I could ask a question about my parents' plants. Lord knew Inez knew a thing or two about gardening.

Inez opened the door and greeted me with a smile. "Ziva, you're right on time." She held the door for me to come in. "Now we have a full table for Bridge!" I looked over her shoulder and saw two older ladies sitting at the kitchen table. "Although, I'd appreciate it if you'd call me back in the future," she added under her breath.

Nooooo, Inez's afternoon bridge game. I tried to hide the look of horror on my face. It looked like my curiosity had finally caught up with me, and I'd be paying for it all afternoon.

THE LADIES DIDN'T CARE that I had no idea how to play the game. I had no clue how many cards I was supposed to have, what trump was, or even how to bid. It was a little hard to focus on the game's rules with Inez rambling away, and us being surrounded by the hundreds of flowers that adorned the walls of her crazy floral-motif kitchen. Inez's kitchen sported sunflower wallpaper, pink rose dish towels, and framed puzzles she told me she was proud to have completed. One was a yellow and red tulip field, and another one an explosion of lavender plants in bloom. The only thing her décor had in common was flowers. It was a decorative collage in the worst sort of fashion. Even the cards we were playing with, and Inez's blouse, were adorned with blooms. I was happy when Inez's friend Doris complained of the heavily perfumed floral air freshener, and Inez reluctantly agreed to unplug it. "But, I love the smell of lilac!" It was almost enough to have me take a sinus pill.

Eventually, through all the flower madness, I managed to get the game's basics down. After we were into the second hand, Inez finally took a breath from talking about planning the church bazar and who had recently died, and I could say, "So, I couldn't help but notice your visitor this afternoon."

"You saw Tico, did you?" Inez said.

"Tico?" I asked.

"Well, I guess he goes by Vincent now, but he'll always be my little Tico," Inez said.

Vincent Delgado was Inez's grandson. Well, wasn't that interesting?

"So, that's why you came running over. I told you he was a looker. I bet now you want me to set you up. You just say the word and I'll call him. How about I call him right now? Maybe I can get him to join us for some tea. Oh, but you kids don't have tea now, do you? No, you probably drink that fancy coffee. What's it called? Cappuccino. We didn't have any of those trendy coffee houses when we were younger. Who wants to sit around and drink coffee anyway? I bet you probably want to go out dancing. Isn't that what we used to do back in the day, ladies?" Inez's friends nodded their heads. "It's a shame he couldn't join us for our game. I asked him to, but he already had plans, probably at the office. He works too hard. I can tell you that. The stress is starting to show in his eyes. He needs a vacation, but I know he won't take one, so I don't say anything. I wish he would though."

I was getting used to Inez's ramblings. I knew that if I just let her keep talking, eventually she'd stop and I could ask a question.

"What does he do?" I asked at the first opportunity. I wondered how much Inez knew about Delgado's work.

"He's an entrepreneur, like you, and such a sweet boy." I doubted he was anything like me. Smuggling goods and selling makeup weren't exactly synonymous entrepreneurships.

Inez continued, "He takes care of me, that he does. He feels the need to protect me and, good heavens, I can't imagine why."

Maybe because he's a super corrupt businessman with plenty of enemies? I thought.

"Tico bought me my car, my condo, even my new washer and dryer, even though there was nothing wrong with the old ones. He said he wanted to be proactive, that's the word he used, and not have my washer go out on me when I least expected it. After my dear Miguel passed away, Tico insisted on taking care of me, and that he has. He promised his grandpa he would and he has kept his word above and beyond what I could ever ask of him. This grandma has no complaints. Every time he stops by, he makes me smile. I tell you what, I am truly blessed."

"You could say that. I'd be happy if I could just get my grandson to go to church, but Lord knows that ain't gonna happen," Doris said. "Yours not only goes to church, but picks you up for it, too, and takes you out for brunch." Everyone nodded as if that sealed it. Delgado was the best grandson ever.

Inez misread my incredulous expression. "See, I told you. You two have so much in common, being in business the way you are, and you're both such sweethearts. I'm sure you would hit it off in a heartbeat," she said.

"If you go out, make sure he takes you to Inez's," added Claire, our fourth Bridge partner.

"Inez's? What am I missing?" I asked. I was sure they didn't mean come back over here for dinner. At least, that's what I was hoping. Dinner with Delgado and Inez would make it the longest date of my life, and I'm not sure I could've handled that, or ever wanted to.

"It's the name of his restaurant," Doris whispered.

Seriously? Delgado owned a restaurant as well, and named it after his grandma? That was just great. Detective Brandle's prime murder suspect turned out to be Grandson of the Year. I wondered if Inez knew about the strip club, and what she thought of it. I didn't dare bring it up and tarnish the image of her beloved grandson, or embarrass her among her girlfriends. Had we been alone, I would've chanced it. Not today though. Plus, I'd have to explain how I came about the information or make something up. Basically, it required me to think it through a bit more before I divulged my secrets.

After listening to Inez go on and on, it seemed hard to believe that Tico and Vincent Delgado were the same person. I couldn't see how a church-going, grandma-loving boy could be a mafia-running murderer. This was the type of story that true crime journalists loved to get their hands on. I'd probably find Delgado's double-life more entertaining, had he not been threatening mine. Delgado was turning out to be one man I wanted to meet for myself, but not on a date. No, I was meeting him on my terms, preferably in a group setting.

Wait, that's it!

In a stroke of sheer genius, I knew just what to do.

"Inez, do you think Vincent's working tonight?" I asked.

"Oh, I'm sure he is. He doesn't think that restaurant of his can survive a Friday night without him. I've told him countless times that it can, but he doesn't listen to me one bit. Thinks he has to be there every weekend. I told him to take Mondays off then, but he told me he can't do that either."

Perfect. There was no time like the present for a girls' night out, and I knew just the place to go.

14

*G*ood heavens, could those ladies play Bridge. I was sure Inez loved playing bridge as much as she loved talking about her grandson. In fact, over the course of the three hours I was there, I believe she told me everything about Delgado—from the time he was born, up until he stopped by her house that afternoon. We talked about where he went to college, where he had lived, his first failed marriage (which of course, wasn't his fault), his beautiful daughter, whom I believed was the only person Inez loved as much as Delgado, and even where he loved to vacation. The man owned a Caribbean island, for cripes sake. Inez told me everything she could think of to make me want to date him, everything except what I really wanted to know. As soon as I was out Inez's front door, I had Aria on the phone.

"Hey, girlie, you got any plans tonight?" I asked.

"Not yet, what's up? You thinking about hitting the town?" she asked.

"Thinking about it. There's this new restaurant I want to try out in Savannah, and then I was thinking about getting some drinks. You down?" I was counting on Inez being right, and that Delgado would be at the restaurant. If not, Aria and I would be hitting the strip club after dinner. I decided ahead of time that I'd fill Aria in on the plan later, after it had been a success. I was worried she go all parental on me if I told her about Delgado and his reputation, and what I expected he was guilty of.

"Should be. Let me call my mom and see if she minds if Arjun spends the night. Do you care if I invite Sasha? She's been wanting to go out for ages, and I keep blowing her off." Sasha was Aria's crazy girlfriend. The one who never turned down a good time. Ever. Let me put it this way, if the bar had a mechanical bull, she was riding it. Come to think of it, Sasha's antics would provide the perfect distraction for me to freely scope out Delgado.

"No, that's cool. See if she wants to come along," I said.

"Okay, I'll text you and let you know what's up. If it's all good, we'll probably be at your place around eight," Aria said.

"Sounds good, girlie. I'll talk to you later." I hung up the phone and checked the time. Six o'clock. *Perfect timing.* I had just enough time to get home and get diva'd up. Vincent Delgado better watch out because, tonight, Ziva Diaz is rolling into town.

"DANG, girl. You're pulling out the big guns tonight." It was quarter after eight, and Aria and Sasha had just pulled up in Raja's red sports car.

"We're going out in style. Love the dress, by the way," Aria said, and laughed. I was wearing her peacock-blue poppy print dress that had the tendency to fall off my shoulder. What can I say? Showing a little skin never hurt. I was hoping the dress would hold Delgado's attention and get him to forget my crazy behavior earlier that day.

"I knew you'd like it. The shoes are all mine though." Against my better judgment, I wore a pair of silver-spiked heels that did fabulous things for my legs. My ex used to love them, which should've been my first clue to switch them out, but no man was worth ditching a pair of heels, even if I knew my feet would kill me come morning.

Sasha slipped into the backseat, literally. I would've gladly moved the seat for her, but she just scooted on back and disappeared between the seats, showing off her red undies in the process. That was Sasha for you.

"Talk about loving the dress," I said. Aria looked gorgeous in a red satin dress and cork heels. Thick spiral curls framed her face and cascaded down her back. Aria had done the opposite of me, and played up her lips instead of her eyes. She wore a chocolate-raspberry-colored lipstick with a gold-tinted lip gloss that gave her pucker a sparkly shine. The shade matched perfectly with her fourteen-carat polished nails.

"Look out, Savannah. We're looking hot tonight!" Sasha said. I had to agree with her, even if I could have done without her silver sequined slip dress. At least she'd be easy to find on the dance floor, or she could fill in for the disco ball if the one at the club broke.

We pulled up in front of the Inez's just before nine. The restaurant was housed in a renovated warehouse in downtown Savannah, a couple blocks up from River Street. Silver-plated doors with *Inez's* etched on the front, told us we were at the right place. When we walked in, I was taken aback by the beautiful artwork and warm interior. Vibrant paintings and striking black-and-white photographs set off the exposed red brick walls, creating a much more intimate atmosphere than I had expected. Overhead, an intricate glass-blown chandelier made me stop and stare. I couldn't get over the explosion of red, orange, and yellow glass flowers. It looked like a summer bouquet on steroids.

Sasha giggled and I looked over at her to see what was up. Of course, she had to find that one painting that looked the slightest bit provocative, and point it out. It's not like you could really see anything. The style was abstract, of course; but if you used a little bit of imagination, it made you wonder if the man was really clothed at all. Perhaps we shouldn't have invited Sasha. Inez's was a classier place than I had expected. There was no mechanical bull.

I gave the hostess my name and we followed after her. I purposely bypassed the main dining room when making our reservation, and requested a table in the lounge instead. I figured I'd have a better chance of catching Delgado's eye closer to the bar. On this side of the restaurant, the lighting was softer and the seating a little more intimate. We weaved our way through the red island-like couches and black armless chairs to a high-backed booth right across from the bar. We couldn't have asked for a better table.

An attentive waiter stopped over and we ordered a round of Cosmos, otherwise known as the official girls' night cocktail. There's just something fabulous about sipping a Cosmo with your girlfriends. I hadn't seen Delgado yet, but the night was young.

Conversation started flowing about the same time the cocktails did. We ordered dinner after finishing the first round. I decided to try the seafood paella. It couldn't possibly be as good as my mother's; then again, I'd yet to find any restaurant that came close to my mother's version. I had high standards in the paella department. Inez's proved to deliver on the drinks, but I wondered how they stacked up on the food. Sometimes, it seemed like the fancier the place, the higher the prices and the skimpier the portions. Or, worse yet, the chef tried to be too innovative and the food combinations tasted terrible. I prayed that wasn't the case. I was starving.

We sipped on our Cosmos and talked about men while we waited for dinner. Sasha had us cracking up, talking about this new guy she was dating and his obsession with golden showers. "Have you ever tried to pee while having sex, it's next to impossible! You got pee splattering all over the place, running down your legs. The cleanup takes forever," she was saying.

"You're crazy. There's no way I'm peeing on anyone near my bed or anywhere else for that matter," Aria said.

"Girlie, you need to get yourself some rubber sheets," I said.

"Oh, no, he has those." The look on Sasha's face was so serious, we totally lost it.

Our laughter drew the attention I was looking for. I looked up and saw our waiter coming across the lounge area with another round of Cosmos, even though we each still had half a drink in front of us. "Compliments of the gentleman behind the bar," he said. We turned our heads to see our suitor. Vincent Delgado was busy mixing up a cocktail, but he stopped long enough to give us a head nod and smile. Well, wasn't this perfect.

"I saw him first," said Sasha.

Aria pick up her half-full Cosmo and said, "Oh no, you've got shower boy." She spoke while looking across the lounge and making eye contact with Delgado. Aria gave him a sexy smile and slowly brought her drink up to her lips. Delgado couldn't stop staring. She held his gaze over the rim of her glass and finished the drink with one long sip before casually setting the glass back down on the table. Zing. With that one look, I knew any advances I had been planning would be pointless. That was okay. As long as he was interested in one of us, my plan would work. Aria would be more than willing to dish the details, if I could just fill her in on the mission ... well, maybe I'd gloss over a couple of the dicer points. I just needed her to get a read on him. She was as good a judge of character as I was. None of that mattered, though, because I couldn't tell Aria any of it, with Sasha sitting with us. I'd have to wait until Sasha went to the bathroom, and give Aria the quick rundown.

"You still got it," Sasha said to Aria. "If he's got a brother, you'd better hook me up." Sasha gazed over at Delgado, but he didn't give her a second glance. I wanted to tell Sasha that he was an only child. Inez, after all, never mentioned anything about a brother, and I'm sure she would've if he did have one.

The next move was Delgado's, and he seized his chance a couple of minutes later by stopping by our table. "Hello, ladies. How are you doing tonight?" he asked.

Aria batted her eyes and offered a sexy smile. "We're fabulous."

I smiled in agreement, bypassing my crazed expression from earlier today for a more natural look, or at least that's what I hoped.

"You look familiar. Didn't I see you this afternoon?" Delgado asked me.

I was waiting for this. I paused for emphasis and pretended to "think" about it. "Oh my gosh. You're right. That was you. Thanks again for your help. I really appreciate it." My voice came out a little too sweet. Aria caught on to it right away.

"You two know each other?" Aria was looking for an introduction and eyeing me for more of the story.

"Sort of. He helped me with a runaway trash can this afternoon at my parents' place. Vincent, correct?" I said.

"That it is," he replied.

"I'm Aria." Aria wasn't about to waste any time getting to know the man. One thing you had to love about her, when she saw something she wanted, she went right for it. It was a trait that both of us possessed, which was probably why we were best friends. "These are my girls: Ziva and Sasha."

I waved a little hello. Sasha snorted.

Luckily, Vincent ignored her. "Nice to meet you. I'm glad you stopped in," he said. I was sure he was only talking to Aria.

"So are we." Aria couldn't have oozed out more sexual charm if she tried.

"I'm not sure what you ladies have planned this evening, but I'm hosting a private reception in the gallery upstairs if you'd like to join me," Delgado offered. Aria didn't even look to us before answering that we would love to. "Great. Well, I see Ricardo is bringing out your dinner. I'll leave you to enjoy it, and I'll stop by afterward."

"Sounds good," Aria said.

As Delgado walked away, Sasha squealed with delight. "Oh, a private party. Aren't we VIPs?" I prayed Delgado was out of earshot.

"You didn't tell me you knew the hottie," Aria said.

"I didn't recognize him," I lied.

"Sure, you didn't." Aria knew something was up. I tried to convey telepathically that I'd fill her in later. I eyed Sasha, hoping Aria picked up that *she* was why I wasn't saying anything. Aria must have gotten my message because she dropped the subject.

I take back my previous comment about the paella. Sorry, Mom, but Inez's recipe was amazing. It was creamy and spicy, with a little salt. In other words, perfect. And they didn't skimp on the shrimp. The seafood in Savannah was truly delish. Maybe next time I'd be brave and try the raw oysters like Aria had. She said the secret to stomaching them, for novices, was bread and garlic butter. I'm all for butter, but I don't know if I could get past the texture. Slime wasn't a characteristic I was a fan of, especially when it came to my food. Aria happily poured them in her mouth off the shell, while I gagged on her behalf. I wasn't an adventurous eater.

Sasha topped both of us, though, in the way she went to town on her prime rib. She looked to be the most eager out of any of us to head up upstairs to the party. I doubted it was any type of party she'd ever been to. I hoped she wouldn't be disappointed by martinis and jazz.

"Girl, you'd better not choke on that. I'm not giving you the Heimlich maneuver, not in these heels," I said to Sasha. Aria laughed. "I'm just saying, slow down. It's good to keep a man waiting every now and then. We don't want to look too desperate. It's not like Del—, I mean, Vincent's going to resign his invitation. Speaking of which, he hasn't been able to take his eyes off Aria since stopping over here."

"What can I say?" Aria was far too pleased with herself.

I had to admit, I was pretty pleased myself. I couldn't ask for the evening to go any better. I was curious who else we might run into upstairs, or what details the night would reveal.

In no time, Ricardo was stopping by to see if we'd like anything else. "Perhaps another drink to take upstairs?" he offered.

"Sure, a vodka martini? Extra dirty," Aria said.

"So, it's going to be like that, huh?" I said to Aria with a smile. "I'll take a gin martini, thanks," I replied to Ricardo.

"You guys got Bud?" Sasha asked.

Oh brother. Sasha had very little couth sometimes.

Delgado brought our drinks over. He didn't even need to ask whose was whose. *Smooth.* "How was your dinner?" he asked.

"It was excellent. Thank you," Aria replied.

"You ready to join me upstairs?" he asked.

"What do you say ladies, are we ready?" Aria asked.

"Lead the way," I replied.

We followed Delgado back out toward the reception area, but turned left down a short hallway, as opposed to turning right to head toward the doors. He paused in the hallway and I wondered what he was waiting for, until the wall's wood paneling slid back to reveal an elevator door. I would've never guessed an elevator was there at all.

"Every month, I host a gathering for friends and business acquaintances," Delgado explained has he punched in a security code to make the elevator operational. "It's a way for me to catch up with everyone all at once, and remind myself to have a good time every now and then." *Maybe Delgado is taking his grandmother's advice after all*, I thought, as the doors slid shut and we headed up.

The elevator opened to a beautiful black-and-white-marbled reception hall. Inside, we were greeted by every socialite who lived within a hundred-mile radius. Of course, my mind went straight to work. I couldn't believe the networking possibilities. This was an entrepreneur's dream. Sasha, already managing to slam her first beer, was headed over to the bar for another, and Delgado and Aria were walking hand-in-hand toward a more-private seating area in the back. I wasn't worried about Aria. She was a smart girl and could hold her own. Like I said, I trusted her instinct just as much as my own, and I was sure she'd give me her read on him later.

"Ziva, crazy running into you here," a pretty blonde said to me.

It took me a minute to place the face. "Kitti?" I didn't recognize her, clothed and without her gold tassels. "You work at Inez's too?" I asked.

"Only at these parties. It helps bring in a little bit of extra cash, and I get to keep my clothes on. Piece of cake," she replied. "I was going to call you. The girls and I have been thinking of having one of those beauty parties. Pamper ourselves, you know? Plus, I could use some new makeup for home. My stuff seems to get ruined at the club," she said.

"That'd be awesome. Give me a call and we'll set something up," I said.

"Okay, the club's closed Sundays, so maybe some time then?" she asked.

"For sure," I said. "And speaking about the club, I forgot to ask you, did Delgado know that Ann Marie and Roger were together?" I had been working on a theory in the back of my mind and it was starting to come together.

"Did he know? Yeah, of course. Delgado knows everything that happens at his club. I think he's the one who hooked them up."

"Really?"

"He saw the way Roger looked at her and, next thing you know, they were together. I always thought it was bad business to hook up with the clients, but not Delgado. He knew how to keep his high rollers happy," she replied.

"Roger spent a lot of money at the club?"

"Oh yeah. His nickname was Big Daddy because he dropped those big bills. Of course, Ann Marie got most of them, but sometimes he shared the wealth. Listen, I have to make my rounds, but maybe I'll see you later tonight," Kitti said.

"Later?"

"At The Palms. That's usually where the after party ends up. I'm due on stage around one o'clock. I'm debuting a new act," Kitti said with a sly grin. I could only imagine.

"Yeah, okay cool. Maybe I will."

Kitti left to go sling drinks and I wandered around the room, pretending to appreciate the artwork. What I was really doing was thinking about the case. I figured no one would give me a second thought if I stared at a painting versus standing slack-jawed in the middle of the room.

While I examined a beautiful real-life Degas and Renoir, I sorted out the facts. Three things I knew for sure. One, Roger was screwing over Delgado. Two, Delgado knew about Ann Marie and Roger. Three, both Roger and Ann Marie were dead. While I couldn't prove it, I was also betting that Ann Marie knew Roger was embezzling funds from Delgado. If *I* knew this, I'm betting Delgado did too. It seemed his motivation for offing the two, kept getting stronger and stronger.

"Excuse me, are you Ms. Diaz? Vincent's lady friend tells me you're the one I must talk to." I turned toward the silver-haired woman. Over her shoulder, Aria caught my eye and smiled. "I'm Ms. DeVine," the woman said, "and I hear you're a beauty expert."

Turns out, Ms. DeVine was looking to turn back the aging clock and hoped I had the magic formula, which, if you asked me, I did. I told her all about Beauty Secrets' rejuvenating line, showcasing my smooth complexion as proof. Truth be told, I probably had my Grandma Diaz's awesome genes to thank more for my wrinkle-free face, but the peptides in Beauty Secrets' formula couldn't have hurt either.

I was beyond thrilled to gain a client like Ms. DeVine. She would be my ticket into the socialites of Savannah. It turned out, her sister-in-law was the Lieutenant General's wife, and her niece was Little Miss Georgia. *Sweet sugar, I would just love to break into the pageant business. Talk about being at the right place at the right time.*

The women who lined up to talk with Ms. DeVine were amazing. Spending an hour within her social circle garnered me more contacts and private consultations than I had earned hosting all my parties last year combined. The rich knew what it took to keep themselves looking young, and they were willing to pay top dollar to achieve it. Good thing I had brought my phone with me, as I was able to schedule several appointments and enter in all the ladies' contact information on the spot. My schedule was packed tighter than a beauty queen in a corset, and I couldn't have been happier. What's more, if I did decide to take my business private, which I was really leaning that way, I might have just met my first investors. The night was getting better and better. Delgado knew what he was doing in hosting these private events. I was already willing to look past a transgression or two.

I looked up just in time to see Sasha staggering my way. Who knew how many beers she'd downed, but it was one too many. I needed to excuse myself before Sasha reached us and said who knows what.

"Excuse me, ladies. It was a pleasure meeting all of you, but there's someone I must catch before she leaves. I'll be in touch soon if I don't make my way back over tonight." I waved goodbye and reached Sasha before she could join the conversation and embarrass us. Oh my, she was drunker than drunk.

"Lookie what I got." Aria's car keys dangled between her fingers. Good Lord, what was Aria thinking giving Sasha the keys?

"I don't think so," I said. I swiped the keys from her hand.

"Hey! I wanted to drive. Aria gave me the keys! You're not being fair." Sasha was starting to act like Arjun. That is, a five-year old.

"Where'd they go?" I asked Sasha.

"Where'd who go?"

"Aria!" Sasha was mentally two steps behind me.

"I dunno. Who cares?" Sasha made a move for the keys and I tossed them in my purse.

"Sasha, come on. What did she say?" I asked.

"Huh?" Sasha was off in Lala Land, scoping out the bartender.

Aria texted me a second later. *Headed to The Palms. Meet you there?* she wrote.

Right behind you, I replied.

DON'T LET SASHA DRIVE! she texted back in all caps.

No worries there. I looked up and Sasha was headed back toward the bar. *Are you kidding me?*

"Hey-ya," she started to whine when I caught up with her and pulled her away.

"C'mon, girl, we got another party to go to," I said.

"We do? A party? Really?" Sasha got way too excited. It was like dangling a chocolate chip cookie in front of a preschooler.

"Yep, and this next one's right up your alley." I just prayed tonight wasn't amateur night.

"Uno minuto," Sasha replied. I gave her a look that said

we didn't have the time. "Promise, just one minute," she said.

I waited, not so patiently, for Sasha to go back up to the bartender. I wasn't sure what she was doing until he handed her a pen. Instead of writing her number down on a napkin, like a sane person, she scribbled her digits on his forearm. The poor guy. At least he seemed amused.

"Let's go," I said, pulling her away once more. "You can hit on the next bartender."

"Oh, good idea!"

No, it wasn't. But it worked. Sasha finally gave in and we were able to leave.

Within five minutes, we had the car back and were headed to the club. We would've been on the road sooner, but Sasha insisted on putting the convertible top down, and there's only so much arguing I'm prepared to do with a drunk girl. At least she didn't ask again to drive.

he party at The Palms was in full effect when we arrived. The doorman unclasped the red rope before we even made it to the door, and didn't say a word about a cover charge. Aria texted me on the way to say they were upstairs in the VIP lounge. I looked up and, sure enough, she and Delgado were sitting on a red-velvet couch, sipping champagne with the rest of the elite. It looked like the no-alcohol law only applied to public areas and not private lounges. Sasha would be happy. That was, if I could find her. The minute we walked in, she disappeared, and I wasn't about to start a search party. I didn't have time to babysit her anyway, if I was going to get to the bottom of who the real Delgado was. My plan had been to join the party upstairs, but I found myself distracted by a particular guy sitting at the bar. I tapped him on the shoulder. "You're so busted."

Finn froze and turned around with a smile on his face. "Yep, you caught me," he said.

"I knew it! You're a regular here, aren't you?" I was

joking, but tried to act serious. It was hard, seeing how I was so happy to see him, my smile was a dead giveaway.

"Oh yeah, a real regular." Finn motioned to a group of about ten guys sitting around a cluster of tables they had pulled together. It was a classic stag party. Not as scandalous as I thought. I recognized the groom-to-be as Chris from the marina. He had a pair of handcuffs clasped on one wrist and a plastic ball and chain around his ankle. His shirt read *Life sentence.* I had to admit, it was pretty funny, and classier than the plastic penises and condom veils that dominated most bachelorette parties. "Why don't you come over and say hi, meet the rest of the guys?" Finn said.

I followed Finn over to the table and offered Chris my congratulations. Finn started introducing his friends, but then I spotted Sasha, and, oh boy. Let's just say, my attention was only on her. She was locking tongues with a beefy-looking bouncer right up against the bar. Bald head, pierced ears, black muscle shirt, and all tattooed up. The bouncer looked like the type of guy you didn't want to mess with. Half the patrons' eyes were locked on them, as opposed to the dancer performing on stage.

"Sorry." I turned my attention back to Finn.

"She a friend of yours?" he asked.

"You could say that." I looked back at Sasha one more time. She and the bouncer had come up for air and were now hitting the dance floor. Seeing she was safe, I rejoined Finn's conversation and met the rest of his friends. They all seemed like cool guys, and didn't care that I was crashing their party.

"I've been meaning to ask you if you wanted to work out together again," Finn said, when it was just the two of us talking again.

I thought about our last attempt at running together and

wasn't sure if I wanted to go there. "We could, or we could do dinner. I make a mean tater-tot casserole," I joked. "Besides, I still owe you for helping me fix up the apartment."

"Nah, you don't owe me anything, but I'll take you up on dinner," he said.

I knew I shouldn't have been flirting with Finn like that, without knowing who the other woman was, but I couldn't help it. He was so dang cute and I just wanted to forget about her, for tonight anyway.

The pulse of the music changed, and the club's lights glowed purple. Finn and I both looked to the stage in time to see Kitti strut out, with a boa around her neck and a sexy safari outfit covering her fanny. The boa wasn't the type with feathers, rather, a real-life albino boa constrictor. The snake glowed white under the club's black lights.

"Sweet sugar, what is she going to do with that snake?" I asked. Finn's eyes widened and he mumbled something about hating snakes.

As it turned out, Kitti allowed the snake to crawl all over her naked body and touch her in places I was hoping no animal had gone before. It was sexy and dangerous at the same time. The audience fed right into it. Well, everyone except Finn. His eyes never left the snake, until one of the bouncers took it backstage so Kitti could work the pole and collect her tips, which were insane, by the way. I could see how these women made a decent living just working a couple nights a week.

Kitti left the stage, and the lights turned red with giant white stars shinning down on the floor. The next girl's act was all-American. It ended with red, white, and blue sequins covering her cha-cha and sparklers shooting out of the floor, to boot. Now, that was creative. The guys hooted and hollered to that one, and I wasn't sure whose act they liked more.

The DJ took over the jams after that, and club goers took to the dance floor to shake it. Sasha was one of the first ones out there again, Beef Stick in tow, of course. I tried not to watch or be embarrassed by her moves. I wondered if Aria was catching all this. We'd have lots to talk about tomorrow.

A couple of the girls, who remembered me and Finn from before, stopped by to say hi. One girl in particular, Tara, dropped off a round of drinks and started talking to me about beauty business. I told her about Kitti's plan to book a party, and she thought it was a great idea. The night had turned out to be successful in more than one way. It was surreal to think about how much my business could grow within the next couple of weeks. The desire to focus on my business made me even more determined to solve the case. I couldn't concentrate on work if someone was threatening me all the time. Paranoia couldn't be good for business.

"So, dinner?" Finn asked again.

Yes, dinner. I was going to suggest tomorrow night, but then remembered my plans with Eric. *Too many men!* I screamed at myself. At that moment, I didn't want anything to do with Eric. Not even for my business. I just wanted to focus on getting to know Finn, and see what developed. Just from spending the last few days with him, I knew he had a good heart, which counted for a lot in my book.

Finn and I were now facing one another, our knees almost touching. I forgot all about Eric and every other man who had ever been in my life. Finn and I were dangerously close to taking our friendship to the next level. I could tell he wanted to kiss me, and I wanted him to. Instead of waiting for him to make a move, I just went for it. Our lips met and I had to remember where we were, or we would've put Sasha and Beef Stick's make-out session to shame.

Out of nowhere, my hair was yanked back and a woman screamed something fierce. I whipped around with my fist in the air and clocked Justine right in the face. If there was one thing I knew how to do, it was fight. She had a wild look in her eye as she lunged at me, claws out, ready to scratch my face off. Finn grabbed her by the back of the shirt.

"Justine, what the hell are you doing here?" Finn yelled.

In the craziness of the moment, it took me two seconds to catch up. So much for forgetting about the mystery woman tonight. Here she was, standing right in front of me. The way she was acting, she had to be Finn's girlfriend. *I knew it.* I almost felt bad for punching her in the face, until I remembered all the crap she had been pulling lately. I wasn't sure who I should be angrier at, her or Finn.

"Wait, Ziva, don't give me that look. Justine's my *ex*-girl-friend. My crazy, psychotic ex-girlfriend," he said, the last part directly to her face. While I didn't disagree with him, I also didn't think it was a smart thing to say, knowing how psycho she could be.

"Baby, you know we're going to be together. I don't understand why you fight it," Justine said.

"You and me together? Not happening. You don't listen. I don't even like you." Finn was harsh. He couldn't have been any more direct than that. "Stop following me. Get a life. Leave my friends alone." I could feel people's eyes on us. It was a good thing Beef Stick was busy, or we'd probably have been kicked out for starting drama.

"But, Finnie, I love you." And then the tears started flow-ing, and then the snot, and then the mascara. Good grief, Justine was a hot mess. I dug around in my purse for a makeup remover towelette. I handed the wipe to her, along with a trial-sized lipstick, and pointed her toward the bathroom. She apparently had forgiven me for punching her upside the head, and readily accepted them.

Finn asked me if I was okay, and I assured him I was.

"Sorry about that. Justine's completely unhinged," he said.

"Oh, believe me. I know." I said it mostly to myself.

I couldn't help but hope that drama didn't regularly follow him around, because I wasn't sure I wanted to be involved in it. Finn must've seen the doubt on my face and hoped to erase it, because he pulled me close to him and kissed me until I was seeing stars.

"That's how our first kiss should've gone," he said.

I didn't answer. My lips tingled better than a sugar rush. I was ready to leave the club, and take Finn home with me.

I kissed Finn back and was liking this getting-to-know-you game, when I looked up and saw Sasha doing her best to swing around a pole. It wasn't pretty.

"Weee! Look at me. I'm a pole dancer," she squealed. Beef stick laughed from below. For a bouncer, he was doing a piss-poor job of keeping the patrons in order.

"You like that?" Sasha yelled down to Beef Stick. Holding onto the pole, she attempted to do a backbend, but Sasha wasn't flexible and I knew what was going to happen a second before it did. She had tipped back too far, causing her heel to slip, and she cracked the back of her head on the dance floor. I was up on the stage, holding Sasha's head in my lap, before Beef Stick and Finn even knew what happened.

"Get some ice!" I yelled down to Beef Stick.

"Sasha, you okay, girl?" I asked. She wasn't quite coherent. I searched the club for Aria but didn't see her.

"What do you need?" Finn yelled up to me.

"Get her off the stage," another bouncer hollered.

"Help me get her down," I said to Finn.

"Are you okay to move?" I asked Sasha. And then, she turned her head and threw up all over the stage. It was disgusting. An observer might've thought it was from hitting her head, but they didn't see her drink her weight in alcohol that night. I could only imagine what the ride home was going to be like. Talk about depressing. What a way to ruin the night.

Sasha sat up and turned to me with the goofiest expression on her face. I thought she had gone mental.

"That was awesome!" she said. "Baby, did you see that?" she hollered to Beef Stick, who was just coming back with the ice. I had no idea what part she thought was awesome: hitting her head, or puking all over the place. He helped her off the stage and, before I knew it, their tongues were going at it again. I had to resist my own urge to throw up.

"At least rinse out your mouth," I yelled at her. It was pointless. The workers cleaned up the mess, and the spotlights worked to draw club goers to the opposite end of the club. Up on the corner stages, two girls performed their own coordinated strip tease, and the audience forgot all about Sasha. I had a feeling management had done this before.

Once again, I looked around for Aria, but I didn't see her. The VIP lounge was empty. "Have you seen Aria?" I asked Finn.

"No, I didn't even know she was here."

"She was upstairs with—"and then I didn't even want to say the name.

"With who?" Finn asked.

I ignored his question and went over and interrupted Sasha. "Have you seen Aria?" I asked her.

Sasha opened her eyes and started giggling. "Ziva, this is Tony," she said.

"Hi, Tony. Can you give us a second?" I pulled Sasha away. I could care less what Beef Stick's name was at that moment.

"Hay-ay!" she protested.

"Listen to me for a sec. Do you know where Aria is?"

"I dunno. Probably with her Latino lover. Now can I go? Tony's waiting for me, and I'm going home with him."

"What?! Girl, that's not smart. Use your brain. You don't even know that guy. You can't just go home with him."

"Ziva, chill out. You're like an absolute buzz killer. Little Miss No Fun trying to tell everyone what to do," Sasha snapped.

"You're ridiculous, you know that?"

"You're not my mom. Quit bossing me around." See, like a five-year old. "Listen, I know what I want, and he's going to give it to me. Back off."

Fine. I wasn't going to sit there and keep arguing with the girl. I finally let her go and told her to call me if she saw Aria, or needed anything. I also threw in a couple threats to Tony if anything bad came of my friend, just for good measure. Then I spotted Kitti across the bar, and went over to see if she knew anything.

"Hey, Kitti, question for you," I said.

"Did you see my act?" she asked. The high of her performance still radiated off her.

"Yeah, it was great. But listen, I'm looking for my girlfriend. She was with Delgado. Have you seen them?"

"Oh sure, they left a while ago."

"Really? Where'd they go?" My pulse instantly kicked up a few beats.

"No clue. He called for the limo about an hour ago, and they slipped out back."

An hour ago? Sweet sugar, they could be anywhere.

"One more thing: what's the story with Beef Stick over there?" I asked.

"You mean Tony? He's a sweetheart. You have nothing to worry about."

"Okay cool. Thanks." Last thing I needed was something bad to happen to Sasha too. Not that anything bad was happening to Aria. No, I just let my best friend run off with a murderer. *I'm sure she's perfectly safe.* I was such an idiot.

I checked my phone and was shocked I didn't have any new texts or missed calls. Aria knew better than to just take off on me like that. It wasn't like her. I texted her asking where she was, but she didn't text me right back. I had to step outside to get a signal.

Finn followed me out while I dialed Aria. Her voicemail picked up. "Hey, girl, just wondering where you're at. Call me." If I could've slammed my phone shut, I would've. This was bad. Like, I-was-almost-having-a-panic-attack-figuring-out-what-to-do-next, bad. I apologized to my Nan for being so stupid, and offered up a quick prayer that she'd help me out again and keep Aria safe. I had really screwed up.

"Are you going to tell me what's going on?" Finn asked.

I didn't want to fess up, but I knew I had to. It all came tumbling out. "We met up with Delgado tonight at Inez's and then ended up here, and then one thing lead to another, and now Aria's missing and I'm pretty sure she's with him."

"What? Are you crazy? What were you thinking?" Finn hollered.

I got defensive. "Hey, your opinion of the man isn't the only one I've heard. I wanted to meet him for myself, form my own conclusion."

"How'd that work out for you?" Finn asked.

"Don't be an ass."

I headed toward Aria's car, thinking about where I should go next, but one look at the car told me I wasn't going anywhere.

"Are you kidding me? Aria's going to kill me." All four tires were slashed and the word *SLUT* was keyed into the side. Finn stopped short beside me. "Like you're the poster child of perfect judgment," I said to him. It was a low blow, but he deserved it. *So much for me trying to be nice to Justine the psycho.*

"Listen, I'm sorry. I just know Delgado's bad news, and I didn't want you anywhere near him," he said.

It felt good to know that Finn cared about me. Now wasn't the time for me to get all sentimental though.

"I know, it was dumb of me, but now what?" I said.

"Now we go to Delgado's house," Finn said.

"You know where he lives?"

Finn nodded.

Of course, he knew.

16

I followed Finn and climbed up into his truck. I couldn't do anything about Aria's car now, so I left it where it was and figured I'd call the cops and Aria's insurance company in a couple of hours. I needed to talk to Aria before I made either of those calls.

Finn tore out of the parking lot, and I finally felt like we were making some progress. I bent forward and unbuckled my heels. The shoes' straps peeled back, leaving red bands across my feet. I stretched my feet out and scrunched my toes. It was painfully good, like acupuncture or a deep-tissue massage. My feet no longer throbbing, I could focus on our new plan.

"Where are we going exactly?" I asked.

"Sea Port. Delgado lives on a plantation, not far on the island."

That's right. Inez had told me that. I wasn't surprised. Some of the richest folks flocked there, right along with the tourists. The once-quiet community had become a vacation hotspot, thanks to the beautiful beaches and myriad of professional golf courses. On a good day, it could take an hour to cross the mainland bridge, and that was during the off season. Traffic alone was reason enough to keep my business elsewhere.

But traffic wasn't a problem this morning. We didn't pass a single car on Highway 17 or 278. Boulevards, landscaped with palm trees and car dealerships with pricey cars, were all I could see. Jaguar, Land Rover, BMW, Mercedes—the island had them all. The dealerships weren't flashy though. Every building on the island, including the car dealerships, banks, and even fast food restaurants and big chain stores, were painted in the same earthy palette. The building material of choice was wood, and not a single sign flashed or scrolled. The result was an effortless beauty, an island surround by nature, accepted by nature. Sea Port was crafted, yet organic. A manicured community that wasn't flashy or pretentious.

"He lives in there." Finn motioned across the street to Huntington Plantation. The entrance was set off with giant gray boulders and a cascading fountain. Two low-watt floodlights illuminated the entrance and a white security house. Outside, a uniformed security officer smoked a cigarette and kept an eye on things. He was no Miles. This guard looked like he could do some damage. Sneaking through wasn't an option, at least not with the truck. Finn continued up the road and turned off into a shopping complex, and parked. Tall, full-leafed trees provided our cover.

"Here, throw this on." He reached in the backseat and tossed me a black button-up dress shirt. The fact that the man carried black clothes in his backseat was questionable. I swam in the material, but, even a bit loose, the shirt provided more cover than my bright-blue dress. Finn untucked his own dress shirt and changed out his shoes. I wasn't so lucky.

We pulled out of the parking lot and back onto the road, turning left and heading back toward Delgado's. Finn was careful to keep his distance from the front security entrance, parking at least two hundred yards away on the deserted gravel shoulder. I got out of the truck without a word. Finn's shirt fell past my dress, making it look like I wasn't wearing any pants. I left my silver shoes in the car and met him at the back of the truck. The grass was slick with dew, allowing specks of dirt and gravel to stick my bare feet.

"Let's go in up there." Finn pointed to a section of the plantation's side hedge up ahead. The foliage wasn't as thick, like part of it had died out and hadn't been replaced yet.

I watched in awe as Finn moved along the hedge with military precision. I could tell this wasn't the first time he'd snuck around in the dark. His footsteps were careful, but sure. His body blended with the hedge, using the branches to their full camouflage capability. I was realizing there was a lot about Finn I didn't know. Me? I was just trying not to step on a picker or get branches caught in my hair.

Finn turned and signaled to me, like they do in the movies. Only, I wasn't sure what his finger pointing meant, until he climbed through the hedge. I followed after him. Finn moved slower now, patiently holding back branches and clearing the path. Pine needles and sticks poked at my bare feet, but I couldn't change that. There was no way that I could have done this in heels. My dress and the over-sized shirt were making it difficult enough. I was no expert.

We came through the hedge in someone's backyard. It was beautifully landscaped with white-striped hostas and blooming red roses. The grass was the shade of green that only money could buy and, in the distance, a pool fountain sputtered, making me have to pee. *I should've gone at the club when I had the chance.*

"It should be this way." Finn motioned to his right. I let him lead the way.

The neighborhood was quiet. Air conditioners hummed and sprinklers ticked on the nearby golf course. The homes back here were for the super-rich with helicopter pads, gorgeous pools, and tennis courts. Luckily, none of the neighbors had privacy fences or large tough dogs. I would have to ditch the dress in order to attempt climbing a six-foot-tall fence, especially if a Rottweiler or Pit Bull was chasing me.

"Get down." Finn pulled at my shirt and crouched low to the ground. I ducked, taking coverage behind a lilac bush in full bloom. The sweet scent tickled my nose, and I was terrified that I would sneeze. That could be a disaster, given that I still had to pee. That is, until I heard the voices. Sneezing and peeing became the last fear on the list.

Finn held his finger up to his lips. He didn't have to worry. I wasn't planning on making a sound. I heard the voices again, and what sounded like water splashing, coming from the other side of the hedge. Whoever it was, they were close. I hoped they weren't coming our way to investigate. I tried not to freak out. This would be so bad for business if I got busted. I could see the headline now, *Beauty Consultant Busted for Burglary*, or something to that effect. What if I got pegged for all the other robberies? This was such bad karma. Cautiously, I moved a branch slightly to the left and peered through.

Um, wow, I found Aria. She and Delgado were skinny dipping and doing things that I didn't know you could do underwater. Finn's expression told me he saw it too. I punched him in the arm, and he turned around.

I jabbed my finger at him while mouthing the words, "Stop looking." Finn had a goofy smile on his face.

Suddenly, he looked like he was sixteen. I ignored him and crawled away from the lilac bush, in stealthy moves ... well, as stealthily as possible for me. Aria giggled in an ooh-I-like-that sort of way. I shuddered. This was so wrong. I'd never felt dirtier in my life. Aria and I were close, but not *that* close.

I waited until I was safely past the neighbor's house, and snuck through the hedge, not caring if it was thicker here or not—I needed to escape. I thought, if Finn was smart, he'd follow right behind me. I didn't look back to check. Branches scraped at my arms and legs, stinging and poking my skin. I moved as quickly and quietly as possible, praying I wouldn't walk right into a snake or any other creepy creature. This wasn't the city; you didn't walk barefoot through the brush without getting bit by something. To think, I used to be a Girl Scout. There went my common-sense badge. I couldn't get back to the truck fast enough.

I counted my blessings when I stepped through the other side of the hedge, with nothing worse than a couple bug bites and a few scratches. I shook the extra-large shirt out, ballooning it with air to check for spiders, and ran my fingers through my hair as if lathering it with shampoo. I'm tough and all that, but spiders scared the bejesus out of me. Invisible bugs crawled on my skin, and I frantically brushed them away, jumping up and down in the process. Finn came out of the hedge behind me and laughed at my creepy crawly dance.

"Feel better?" he asked.

"Not really." I examined the scratches on my skin and saw one or two were bleeding. Tonight had been a disaster. And to think, it started out so promising.

"Well, at least you know your friend's okay," Finn said with a smirk as we climbed into the truck.

"Aria's going to kill me once she finds out what I know." Now that I knew she was okay, I was feeling some major guilt.

Finn was silent, and that was smart on his part. I thought about Aria some more. I planned to fess up to her later today and hoped she wouldn't hate me forever. I thought about her car, and I felt even worse. I was becoming more depressed by the minute.

"I have an idea. Why don't we get some breakfast? I'm starving. I know you must be too. Then, we can think about what to do next," Finn said.

I looked at the clock. It was already close to four AM. Aria would be picking up Arjun from her mom's in a few hours, and then I could talk to her. I wouldn't be able to sleep until I did. "Okay, good plan," I said.

Finn drove off the island to a local greasy spoon. It was too early to be busy, but a couple senior citizens occupied a table here and there, mixed in with the all-nighters like us. There was no chai tea on this menu, and I was pretty sure the black coffee would kill me. Not like my nerves needed the caffeine either. Finn, of course, ordered a Coke. I went with the hot chocolate. Chocolate was always good. Chocolate was my friend. I loved chocolate.

"What time do you think the insurance company opens up?" I asked Finn.

"Ziva, I'm sorry about that. Justine's seriously screwed in the head. You have no idea."

"Actually, I do."

Finn's eyebrows rose.

"She's been my enemy since fourth grade, and the universe keeps throwing her my way. I must've done something to piss karma off, because I can never seem to get rid of her. What's your story with her?" I asked.

"We dated a few months back, nothing serious. She was normal when we were together. I had no idea she'd go all psycho when we broke up."

"You must've done something to set her off," I said.

"Thing is, I don't know what. It's not like I cheated on her. It's like, after we broke up, I kept running into her. It took me a while to figure out she was stalking me. When she dropped in on my vacation in Mexico, that was it."

"What? She crashed your vacation? That is crazy ... and sadly, totally like her."

"Oh, it gets better. First, she showed up at the resort, and then, when I told her to get lost, she called Customs and told them I was a drug smuggler." I tried not to laugh, but couldn't help it. "Then when I finally got back to the States, we caught her breaking into Murphy's, trying to spike the cola with a love potion."

"Yeah, she doesn't get over things easily. She's still ticked she didn't make the cheerleading squad in high school, so you're totally screwed," I said with a smile.

"You're telling me. I haven't had a serious girlfriend since her, and I'm pretty sure that even if I moved away, she'd hunt me down and make my life hell. She already tracked me out of the country once."

"I've said it before and I'll say it again. She needs to get herself a boyfriend, and some therapy."

"I thought about that, but I couldn't set her up with anyone I know. The poor bastard wouldn't know what hit him." Finn flagged down a waitress to take our order. Given how slow they were, you'd think the waitresses would've been right on it. I didn't care much, seeing how I had a couple hours to kill, but I was getting hungry. After the waitress left, Finn continued, "Heck, I even have a restraining order on her, but you see how well that worked."

Yeah, about as well as my cease-and-desist letter.

"Well, I'm sure Delgado's got cameras in the parking lot, so we can take that to the police if we want to. Plus, you have all the drama inside. Not sure how much trouble she'll get in, but I'll do whatever I can to help you out." I was just as eager as he was to get rid of Little Ms. Cuckoo, especially if I was going to start seeing Finn on a regular basis.

"Anyway, I'm sorry for what Justine did. I'll talk to Aria for you if you want," Finn offered.

"No, that's okay. I need to talk to Aria anyway." I wasn't sure what I wanted to lead off with. Either: *Hey, you know that guy you hooked up with last night?* Or *Guess what Justine did to your car.* The later might be easier to explain, and I could blame it on someone else.

"You going to tell her about Delgado?" Finn asked.

"I have to. I know she likes him now, but wait until I tell her what I know." Aria liked her fair share of bad boys, but dating a murderer was going a little too far. She was going to be crushed. Not the first time tonight, I prayed Delgado wasn't Detective Brandle's man after all. If he wasn't, though, I had no idea who was. I was getting depressed. If this case went unsolved, I would never feel safe again.

Our food came out and I was grateful. I tucked into my pancakes, after drowning them in syrup, and Finn did the same ... minus the syrup part. We ate in silence, and I'm embarrassed to say that I cleaned my plate. If I had been offered another pancake, I would've eaten that one too. As it was, I was thinking about ordering dessert. Chocolate cream pie sounded divine. Maybe I shouldn't have sworn off working out. *Maybe I shouldn't be such an emotional eater.*

Finn was dropping me back off at home when my cell phone rang. It had to be Aria. I snatched the phone out of my purse and checked the caller ID. I was close; it was her mom.

"Ziva, thank goodness you picked up. I thought it was too early to call, but Aria insisted I did right away."

"Why, what's wrong? Is she okay?" Finn glanced over at me and looked ready to help.

"She's more than okay," Mrs. Rao gushed.

"Oh, thank heavens." I exhaled a shaky breath. I knew Aria was *more than okay* when I saw her a couple hours ago, but anything was possible when Delgado was involved. I wouldn't feel better until Aria was back home and I had a chance to talk to her.

"She was just worried that you didn't get her message last night," she continued.

"She'd be right about that." I had a feeling I had Sasha to thank for that. It would be a long time, if ever, before I hung out with her again.

"I won't keep you sweetie, but Aria just wanted to let you know that she'd be in touch in a couple of days. Her cell phone fell in the pool, or something along those lines. I didn't quite catch the details. She said she'd call you as soon as she could." I could take a wild guess why she bypassed the pool details to her mom.

Then, I thought about what Mrs. Rao had said. It took my sleep-deprived brain a moment to kick in. "Wait, did you say couple of days?" I was in panic mode again.

"Yes! Isn't it wonderful? Last night, her boyfriend surprised her with a Caribbean vacation. I can't even imagine. I'm so happy for her. I didn't even know she was dating anyone, but I'm sure you know all about him."

That I did, and none of it was good.

"Listen, what did she say exactly? Where's Arjun?" Finn

stared at me, trying to figure out what was happening. I relayed the information as fast as I could.

"Arjun's still with me. Aria asked if I'd watch him for a couple of days. As for where they were going exactly, *that* I'm not sure. Aria made it sound like he owned some island, but that couldn't be, now, could it?" Mrs. Rao's voice went up with excitement.

Yes, that was exactly where they were headed, to Delgado's private island. Sweet sugar, my luck, Delgado caught wind of what was about to go down and was fleeing the country before he could get charged, and he had my best friend with him. I had to stop them before they left.

"What time were they leaving? Did she leave a number or anything?" I asked.

"No, why? What's going on, Ziva?" Mrs. Rao asked.

My breakfast rested like lead in my stomach. How was I supposed to tell Aria's mom that I set her daughter up with a murder suspect? I couldn't do it. "Nothing, I just wanted to catch up with her from last night. Did she give you any other details?"

"No, but I'm betting you have about an hour to catch her. After that, it'll have to wait until Wednesday."

17

*F*inn didn't wait for me to give directions. He was already thinking the same thing. We barreled back down the highway toward Delgado's estate, knowing they'd probably depart from his house. After all, what was the point of having your own helicopter pad if you didn't use it?

During the drive, I stared at my phone, willing it to ring. There was no point in dialing Aria's cell, now that I knew it was broken. I thought about how else I could reach her. I flipped through my social media accounts to see what had been posted. A couple of pictures and location check-ins from last night popped up, but nothing since. I left Aria a private message, anyway, telling her that I had talked to her mom this morning and to call me back ASAP and that it was an emergency. I didn't dare go into details in the message, because, who knew who she was with? Last thing I needed was Delgado to know I was on to him.

In between stressing and messaging Aria, I tried to contact Detective Brandle. I hoped he could intervene somehow, arrest Delgado before it was too late, or delay the flight, but he didn't answer his cell or office line. I seriously debated dialing 9-1-1, but had no idea how to explain the situation to the operator without sounding like a total nut ball. I'd waste more time trying to explain the problem than I was afforded. My only prayer was for us to make it to Delgado's before they left, and not get pulled over in the process. The speed at which Finn was driving was sure to land him a ticket and a reckless driving charge, if a cop tagged us.

"So, what's the plan?" Finn asked.

"I don't know. I haven't thought of one. We obviously can't sneak through the bushes in broad daylight, and I don't even have any free samples to pull off a beauty delivery." Come to think of it, the only thing I had on me were the clothes on my back and the contents of my purse. "Wait, I have an idea, but you're going to have to let me drive your truck," I said.

"I'm fine with that, if you think you can get us in," Finn replied.

"I think I can, but don't look for a sec. Keep your eyes on the road." I shouldn't have said that. I should've just went about my plan because, of course, Finn was going to watch me now. I unclicked my seatbelt and, as discreetly as possible, shimmed out of my panties and tucked them in my purse. Thank goodness I had worn my fancy panties, or this plan wouldn't have worked at all. "Now, before we get to the gate, pull over and hop in the backseat and hide. I think my plan will work better if the guard doesn't see you."

"I don't think I want to know what you're planning," Finn replied.

"Don't worry; it's nothing like that," I said.

When we neared Huntington Plantation, Finn pulled

into the same shopping complex as last night and parked, to switch spots and hide in the backseat. At the plantation entrance, I pulled up to the gate and was greeted by the guard. The fact that he was an older man seemed encouraging.

"Good morning, Miss. What can I do for you?" he asked.

"Hi there. I'm here to see a guest of Mr. Delgado's, a Ms. Aria Patel? She asked me to drop off a couple of necessities for their upcoming trip." I pulled the panties out of my purse. "It's a surprise for Vincent," I said with a smile. The guard fumbled with his pen against the clipboard. "I'm just going to make this delivery to her really quick, and then I'll be out of your hair." I took my foot off the brake and inched the truck forward, not giving the guard much time to think.

"Oh, okay," the guard said when he managed to find his voice.

"Thanks so much. Have a good one." I tried not to gas it when the gate lifted, but I knew we were running against the clock.

Finn waited until we were out of sight from the security station, to sit up in the backseat. "Which way?" I asked him. It was a harder than I'd imagined, finding Delgado's estate in the daylight. Huntington wasn't a normal subdivision. The houses were as grand as they built them, with their stone facades, manicured lawns, and circular drives. Even the mail boxes were fancy, with their gold and stone accents.

"To the right. See? We walked through the backyard from the bushes, from the main road," Finn said.

I turned right at the next road and couldn't believe it. This had to be the way to his house. A white brick old-English "D" was inlayed into the pavement, and the entire street leading up to the house was lined with flowering trees. I didn't have time to admire the house's grandeur. I barely registered the porch's white marble columns as I pulled around the circular drive and threw the truck into park behind a limo. Finn started toward the front steps, but I was already heading around back. "Please don't let us be too late, please don't let us be too late," I repeated with each step.

I rounded the corner toward the backyard and was hit with a blast of air, and then I heard the thumping. The helicopter's blade whirled and kicked up the air all around me. The wind grabbed my dress, and I had to fight to keep the silk from being whipped over my head. *Maybe taking my panties off wasn't such a good idea.* Waves rippled across the pool, and everything that wasn't nailed down swayed from the wind, including the patio umbrella. Finn ran on ahead of me, past the tennis court and toward the helicopter pad. I followed him, but we were too late. Within a few seconds, the helicopter lifted off and hovered just above the house.

With one hand on my dress, I waved my other arm above my head as if I were stranded on a deserted island and a rescue helicopter was circling overhead. Heaven help me. It was pointless. Aria wasn't looking at me at all. Up in the window of the second-, or maybe it was third-story, a little girl waved out the window. It took me a second, but I figured the little girl was Delgado's daughter. The one Inez had told me about yesterday. Aria had a huge smile on her face, and blew the little girl a kiss. The girl copied her with the kisses. She must have given her twenty kisses within five seconds. It would've all been very cute, if this hadn't been an emergency.

Finally, at the last possible moment, Aria looked over and spotted me. Even from a hundred feet above us, I could tell she was laughing. I tried to motion for her to come down, but I don't think she realized what I was saying. She waved back and blew me a kiss too. For the love of all things chocolate, Aria didn't get it at all. She must have thought I was there to see them off. I didn't know how well Aria could see me anymore, as the helicopter was starting to gain some altitude, but I held my thumb and pinkie up to my ear in the universal "call me" sign and prayed that she would see it and call me as soon as she could.

The helicopter soared away, taking its hurricane gales with it, and leaving me feeling deflated. The one thing I didn't want to have happen was now smack in my face, and I didn't know what to do.

Finn didn't say anything on the walk back to the truck. There wasn't any point in ringing Delgado's doorbell. It's not like the maid would give me directions to his vacation home, if she even knew where it was. There was a reason why they called them "private" islands.

We got back in the truck and I checked my phone. Detective Brandle hadn't called back, and I wasn't surprised.

"Now what?" Finn asked. I thought things through. First off, I needed to talk to Detective Brandle. I dreaded telling him what I'd done, but I needed his help. He was my best ally. Too bad he hadn't returned my calls yet.

"Do you want to come back and crash at my place for a couple hours?" Finn offered.

I considered it for a minute, but my phone chirped, reminding me about the bridal expo this morning. I gave an audible sigh and knew I'd better get home.

I thanked Finn for dropping me off at home, for the second time that morning, and for everything he had done for me in the last twelve hours. Heck, make that the last week. We had been through a ridiculous amount of drama in our short friendship, and he still hadn't bolted. That said something. I had planned on giving him a quick friendly kiss on the cheek as more of a thank you, but Finn turned toward me and met me with his lips. I could get use to kissing that man. For five seconds, I didn't care about anything else but Finn. It was the best five seconds of my day.

18

*T*he bridal expo was packed, as I'd expected. The spring show always drew in a big crowd. I figured it was from all the newly engaged couples from the holiday, and Valentine's Day proposals. My ex proposed to me on Valentine's Day, too. If it wasn't for all the chocolate candy and discounted champagne, I would now loathe the day. I had been right that Justine would be there too. She had a large vinyl sign hanging behind her booth that said *Wanna know my secret?* I thought it was probably herpes, but no one asked me. I was exhausted, but I put on my happy face and worked my tail off, doing mini makeovers and handing out wedding-day-makeup tip sheets and goodie bags. Mindy from Fancy Cakes was set up right across from me, and kept my sugar rush alive by tossing me a sugar-laced treat every hour. She knew me well.

Finally, around 11 o'clock, there was a break in the action. I took the time to reorganize my table and restock my supplies. I didn't need to look up to know Justine was standing over me.

"You've got some nerve showing up here after last night," I said, without looking up from my bag.

"I don't know what you're talking about." I could hear the satisfaction in her voice.

I reminded myself a handful of times that I was a professional, unless I seriously became unhinged. I thought I had been very patient with Justine, but I was so tired of her crap. "Whatever. You need to move on." I meant that in more ways than one.

"I just wanted stop over and wish you and Finn the best of luck. You were always only good enough for my sloppy seconds."

That was it. I didn't care who was around. I was set to pummel her. But, I didn't have to.

Justine was so full of herself, she tossed her hair over her shoulder and turned around and smacked right into Mindy, who was carrying an industrial-sized tray of gourmet cupcakes. Justine screamed. Cupcakes flew in the air and started raining down on everyone. Justine pushed Mindy, as if it had been her fault, and ended up slipping on the whipped-cream-covered floor in the process. Justine's arms flailed as she tried to catch her balance. She fell backwards and crashed right into the chocolate fondue table. The chocolate fountain went airborne. I ducked for cover as a wave of melted chocolate headed my way. Brides-to-be screamed as chocolate slopped and glopped all over the place. A few seconds later, I peeked up from behind the table and witnessed chaos. Vendors stood open-mouthed in shock. Brides and their friends were completely disgusted at the chocolate in their hair and on their clothes. Me? I had the biggest smile on my face. Sitting on the floor, covered head to toe in chocolate, and pitching a temper tantrum, was Justine. She looked absolutely ridiculous. It totally made my day. I shamelessly took out my cell phone, walked over, and snapped a pic of her. Turns out, karma was on my side after all.

The expo was pretty much done after that. When I got home, I thought about just crawling into bed, but I did have a few chocolate streaks in my hair that I didn't want getting all over my pillowcases. The shower won in the end, but not by much. I was not used to pulling all-nighters. Even my energizing body scrub seemed weak. Grapefruit extract could only do so much to wake the senses. I washed just the necessities, and was toweling off, when the doorbell rang. *Now, who would ring my doorbell on a Saturday afternoon?* The off chance that it was Detective Brandle was enough to propel me into some clothes and make it downstairs to answer the door before the second ring. I should've looked out the peep hole first. It was a mistake I would never make again. To my surprise, Eric was standing on my doorstep, wearing his ever-fashionable suit with a bottle of champagne in his hand and a smile on his face.

"What are you doing here?" It wasn't the most-polite thing to say, but it's what I blurted out. I wasn't ready to see Eric, not when I was still figuring out how to put our relationship firmly in the friendship category. I was wishing I hadn't answered the door. The morning had already been too much.

"I thought we could celebrate," he replied, not faltering for a second. Celebrating was the last thing on my mind and drinking was a close second. "The case is as good as solved. Everyone knows Delgado's their man. Now the cops just have to bring him in," Eric said.

I held the door for him to come in. This was going to take more than a minute to explain.

"About that," I said, "Delgado's actually going to be out of town for a while."

And then, believe it or not, I started crying. I was doing the one thing that I hated when people did it to me. It was embarrassing, but I couldn't stop it once I started. The emotions from the past twenty-four hours had finally caught up with me. Between sobs, I told Eric about what had happened with Aria, and I was thankful that he didn't interrupt or chastise me like others would have.

When I was finished, Eric said, "Well, there's nothing we can do about it now, and you said Delgado will be back on Wednesday, so we'll just have to wait it out until then."

"Aria will be back on Wednesday. I have no idea if Delgado's coming with her or not." If Delgado really was on to us, he wouldn't be coming back for a long time, if ever.

"Well, we'll just have to pray that he does. In the meantime, get in touch with Detective Brandle and see if he can do anything on his end." Eric's matter-of-fact attitude was refreshing. I needed someone to ground me and take control of the situation. Plus, his plan sounded about as good as it was going to get.

"Now, why don't you go get ready and I'll make us brunch," Eric offered. I started to protest about not having any groceries. I hadn't really restocked the cupboards since the break in. "Not a problem. I stopped by the store on my way over. I've been wanting to cook for you, so, why not start with eggs?" I guess I couldn't argue with that. It was a two-breakfast kind of morning anyway, and you didn't kick someone out of your house when they showed up to cook you brunch. My mom had instilled some manners in me, after all.

Bacon sizzled and eggs fried while I pinned up my hair and attempted to conceal my dark eye circles. The makeup would buy me a couple of hours until I could hit the sheets, or risk looking like a zombie.

"Mimosa?" Eric offered when I joined him back downstairs.

"Thanks." I took a seat at the breakfast bar and watched him finish our breakfast.

"Your place looks nice. I heard it was pretty trashed after the break in," Eric said.

"You heard about that?" I asked.

"You know how news travels around here," he said.

Yeah, that I did know. I was just surprised that it had travelled all the way to Savannah.

"Did you still want help digitizing those files?" Eric motioned to a broken and taped binder that had once been my *Beauty Bible.* "I thought about bringing my scanner over, but ... well, I was actually hoping that you'd still want to come over tonight," he said.

"I do need to scan them, but I've decided to pick up my own scanner. I should own one anyway. Thanks again for the offer though."

"What about dinner?" Eric just wasn't going to drop it. I had purposely kept my mouth shut about my plans tonight. Right now, the only man I wanted to have dinner with was Finn.

I went with a half-truth. "I'm going to have to pass on dinner tonight. Last night's drama was a bit much, and I need some time to decompress." No one could argue that I could use some time alone. I was also totally chickening out with the *let's-just-be-friends* conversation, but I was okay with that.

"That's understandable. You've been through a lot lately, what with your apartment being broken into and your ring being stolen," Eric said.

"You know it. But wait, how do you know about the ring?"

"Huh?" Eric turned from the stove.

"My ring, how'd you know it was stolen?" I asked.

"Oh, you know, like I said, news travels around here," Eric said.

"But, I never reported the ring." I should have kept my mouth shut. I blame it on fatigue. The looks on both our faces gave away our thoughts, and we both knew the truth. It was Eric who had broken into my apartment, he who had left the threatening note on my car, and he who had been the one to kill Roger and Ann Marie. *Now what?* I was defenseless in my own home. My flight response kicked in once more, but I fought it. This was the bastard who'd been making my life hell the last few weeks. I refused to run from him.

I switched tactics. Eric liked me, of that I was certain. It was time for me to use that to my advantage. "You know, Eric. I've been thinking, you and me? We're smarter than everyone else." I walked around the counter and approached the stove. Eric looked skeptical. "I don't know why you did it, but it's pretty smart the way you set up Delgado ... and I have to admit, pretty damn sexy. I've got a thing for bad boys." I traced the pearled buttons of his shirt while talking, and leaned into him. My hands rested on his hips.

Eric bought into it. "Do you now?" He trailed his finger down my shoulder, and rested his hand on my waist.

"Mmm hmm. Want to tell me *why* you did it?" I asked.

"You really want to know?" he asked.

I pushed against him. "Do share." Not only did I want to know the truth, but I was trying to buy myself some time, so I could think about what to do next.

It was easier to seduce a murderer than I would've thought. Eric started talking. "It all started when Roger began seeing that stripper. He just couldn't keep his pants on. I couldn't care less who he banged; but when he starting screwing over our clients to pay for his lifestyle, things had to stop."

"But Roger couldn't," I said to encourage Eric on.

"Of course not. Roger didn't know how to say *no* to Ann Marie. He was embezzling funds from clients to pay for his lifestyle, and he was going to ruin us. I'd spent too long building my life, becoming someone, to have it ruined by some whore. So, I took care of it." Eric smiled with satisfaction. I knew exactly what he meant by *taking care of it*. I felt sick. "Roger was the one who screwed over Delgado, so he's the one who paid. But don't worry. No one will ever know it was me. The files, the transactions, they all point to Delgado. As far as anyone knows, he's the murderer." Somehow, I doubted Delgado would go down for a crime he didn't commit. Sooner or later, he'd discover Eric set him up.

Eric turned sympathetic. "I'm only sorry I had to hurt you in the process. You're okay though, aren't you? I tried not to hurt your neck too badly, but you're a fighter." He traced his finger down my jaw bone. "Can you forgive me?"

"Of course," I managed to say, once I found my voice. Eric spun me around so my back was against the counter, and kissed me in reply. I knew I had to act, but I couldn't think. I kissed him back and racked my brain with what to do next. The fear in my body added to the intensity of the kiss. Eric closed his eyes and leaned forward, until my back arched against the countertop. I tried to keep my focus as his hands explored the curves of my body. A thin layer of cotton separated his fingers from my skin. I didn't know how long I could continue this game. I tried to talk, to say anything, or even push him away, but Eric wouldn't stop.

My fingers searched behind me, toward the stove. Eric misinterpreted my actions and bent lower. His weight pushed down on me. The smell of his cologne filled my nostrils, the same as it had that morning in Marion's kitchen, and I wanted to gag. I needed to end this. His hands pushed up my skirt as my fingers found the handle to the pan on the stove. I picked it up and cracked him on the back of the head with it. Eggs and grease splattered the walls and floor, and oozed down the back of Eric's dress shirt. His body fell limp on top of mine. I struggled to push his dead weight off me, and managed to squirm out from underneath him, leaving him passed out on my counter. He didn't twitch or make the slightest sound. I had no idea if I'd killed him or not. Stunned, I dropped the frying pan on the counter and looked up. Detective Brandle stood speechless in my doorway.

19

I sat in the front seat of Detective Brandle's gold Impala while he questioned me. Outside the window, the patrol cars' lights flashed, and an ambulance pulled away from the building. The scene had overwhelmed my senses. I felt calmer without the white and red lights swirling outside the car window. I didn't turn to face Detective Brandle, until the last audible sound of the ambulance's siren faded in the distance. I had no idea how to explain all of this, or where to start. I took a deep breath and gave it a go. Detective Brandle listened while I explained everything that had happened since the break in.

When I finished, Detective Brandle said, "So I take it this belongs to you?" He held up a plastic baggie that contained my ring, along with some other jewelry.

"Yes, that's mine," I said.

"I can't give it back to you yet, but I wanted to let you know that we found it," Detective Brandle said.

"Where?" I asked.

"We went back to SIS this morning with a follow-up warrant, this time focusing on Eric's office. We found your ring, along with plenty of cash and some other jewelry believed to belong to Ann Marie, in his desk. It didn't surprise me when we found it, given his history," Detective Brandle said.

"What history?" Eric mentioned something about building his life, but I just thought he was talking about growing up poor.

"Eric was arrested a half of dozen times when he was younger, for breaking and entering. It looks like he put those skills to use, too, while trying to get the funds back to balance the books."

"Wait, he's the town thief?" I was stunned. I didn't see that one coming.

"He thought he was smart, but he was sloppy. Left prints at Winston's, and used his car to get away after robbing Cognac's."

That was dumb. And he definitely wasn't that smart. Good thing I hadn't given him any money to invest for me. My business dreams could've been gone in a snap.

"What made you start considering Eric?" I asked.

"We would've eventually, as normal protocol, but it was the note he left on your car that propelled the investigation. We got lucky when his print matched. It's when you mentioned Delgado that I started to put all the pieces together."

Turns out, Detective Brandle was a better detective than I gave him credit for. It would've been nice if he could've clued me in to it all.

"What did Delgado have to say?" I was eager to see where this conversation would lead.

"He's really not a bad guy; likes people to think he is, better for his business. He knew Roger was stealing from him, but they worked out a deal. That's why Roger was selling his boat."

"To pay off his debt," I said.

"Exactly," replied the detective.

So, Marion had been right. Roger really didn't have the cash. Looked like he got in over his head with his lavish lifestyle. It also looked like Roger's plan hadn't been good enough for Eric. That, or he couldn't forgive him.

"So, now what?" I asked.

"Now we head down to the station to file your statement. We need all the evidence we can get if we're going to put Eric away for life."

YESTERDAY HAD BEEN A LONG DAY. Between knocking out Eric and spending hours at the police station, I was more than ready to put the day behind me. The next morning was different. I woke with a clear head and a refreshed soul, ready to tackle the day. My product shipment that had been delivered the day before, was ready and waiting to be packaged and delivered. It felt good to be working, and I knew my clients would be happy to have their new summer collections soon. I smiled when I saw all of Aria's nail polishes, and set them aside. Man, I loved that girl. I was beyond thankful to hear Delgado had been cleared. I'd still have to fess up to my original suspicions and, of course, fill her in on her car, but it looked like she and Delgado could have their happily ever after, or however long the relationship lasted.

I thought about how crazy the past week had been, on the drive over to Marion's. Nothing could've prepared me for the last product drop-off at her house. I prayed to never find myself in a similar situation. Marion already had company when I got there, but I decided to pull in anyway. I parked the pickup alongside the other car and grabbed Marion's gift bag, shutting the car door with my hip.

Walking up Marion's driveway, I thought about what a gorgeous day it was. If you could believe it, it was actually cool out. The night before, a rain storm rolled through and brought relief from the heat and humidity. Today, it wasn't supposed to be warmer than seventy-five. I was loving it. It might have been cool outside, but it looked like things were heating up in Marion's doorway. The sight of she and Dr. Michelson embracing in the entryway stopped me short. Marion didn't need my gift bag. The doctor was already adding color to her cheeks with a sweet kiss goodbye. From the looks of it, this wasn't the first time they had shared an intimate moment. I froze, barely hidden behind a Japanese maple tree, and found myself wishing I would've dressed in black. But then again, the dark hue wouldn't have helped me hide on a beautiful day like today.

The front glass door opened and I averted my eyes to the ornamental tree. My fingers automatically traced the delicate leaves, pretending to be consumed by their miniature beauty.

"Good morning, Ziva," Dr. Michelson said. He looked surprised to see me, but wasn't embarrassed.

I copied his expression. "Morning, Dr. Michelson."

"A gift for Marion?" he asked pointing to the bag.

"Just her latest delivery," I said.

"Oh, I was going to say that if it was a present, she doesn't need it. I've given her enough to smile about today."

Oh my. If I was the type who blushed, it would've been at that moment.

"Have a good day," he said with a wink. I was left on

the front porch, speechless. Marion came to the door to investigate, and saw the look on my face. Awkward wasn't an adequate word to describe my feelings. Remembering her manners, Marion opened the security door and invited me in. Charlie came galloping behind her to greet me.

"This is for you." I handed Marion the gift bag and bent down to pet Charlie. "Hey, buddy. You're looking good, much better than last time." Charlie sat against my legs, his stubby tail thumping rhythmically against the floor. His gray muzzle nudged my hand with excitement. He loved the attention, and I gave him my all. I petted him for another minute and then stood up to face Marion.

"How are you holding up?" I asked. Talking about Roger seemed like a safe topic of conversation.

"Good," Marion said, massaging her hands. "The funeral is on Wednesday. Did you see that in the paper?"

"No, I haven't yet," I said.

"Philip sent in the obit. It'll be in tonight's paper too," she added.

I wasn't a read-the-paper sort of gal, but I told Marion I would check it out. It seemed like the polite thing to say. "Do you guys need anything? I can make something for the luncheon if you're having one," I offered. More like I'd buy something, but same difference.

"Oh no, don't worry about it. It's all taken care of. Rich is paying to have it catered."

Dr. Michelson was paying to cater the funeral luncheon? This was all just too weird. I couldn't keep my mouth shut anymore. "What's the story with you two anyway?" I asked.

"It's complicated," Marion replied.

"Yeah, I figured that much out on my own," I said with a smile.

"I guess you have, so I'll tell you this. I've known Rich for a long time. Thought he was the one, but it didn't work out."

"Why not?" They clearly looked head over heels for one another.

"We were young. He was focused on med school, and I didn't want to wait. It was the biggest mistake of my life." Marion's voice was full of regret.

"So, you married Roger and the rest is history?" I asked.

"Pretty much. I married the lying, cheating jerk and lived with my choice for the last thirty years," she said.

"You and Rich never..." I didn't want to say what I was thinking.

"Had an affair? No, I never stepped outside of my marriage. Not that anyone would've blamed me if I had." She was right about that. "No, I still had morals and kept my vows, even if I was the only one."

Wow, that was commendable.

"But, now, things are different. I'm so ready for *now*," she said, and then she started crying. *Gah.* Did I mention how much I hate when people cry? Seriously, nothing makes me more uncomfortable. I never, ever, know what to say. I always feel like such an idiot.

"I'm sorry," she said after a moment.

I walked over and gave her a hug. For once, the right words came to mind. "You deserve to be happy," I said.

Marion used the back of her hand to wipe away her tears. "I don't know why I deserve it any more than the next person, but thank you."

I HAD a lot on my mind after leaving Marion's house. While I drove over to Mrs. J.'s, I thought about Finn and wondered what our future held. The man definitely had potential. It had been awhile since I'd been able to say that about any man. I prayed that I was becoming a better judge of character. I didn't want to have two ex-fiancés.

My cell phone rang as I was getting out of the car. Like usual, Mrs. J. was sitting on her front porch—sweet tea at her side and a piece of pie on the breakfast table—just waiting for a visitor. She was dressed head to toe in black, no doubt already in mourning for the funeral tomorrow. My heart flipped when I looked down and saw Aria calling. It wasn't the best timing, but I had to take it. I turned my back to the porch, but I knew Mrs. J. would still pick up the conversation.

"Girlie, what's up? I've been wanting to talk to you for days," I said.

"Ziva, can you hear me?" Aria's phone was cutting in and out.

"Barely. What's up?" I shouted back. Aria replied, but I couldn't make out what she said. "What? I can't hear you?" Now was not the time for poor reception.

Then her phone became crystal clear as she shouted, "I'm engaged!" I pulled the phone away in shock. Mrs. J. screamed in excitement on the front porch.

"Can you believe it? Engaged!" Aria shouted, "And you've got to see this ring."

"I bet it's amazing." I could only imagine what type of bling Delgado had placed on her finger. I was beyond thankful that he was an innocent man. I didn't want to think about the conversation we'd be having if he wasn't.

I had been planning on telling Aria about her beloved car when she called, but I was not about to spoil her happiness. In fact, I just made up my mind to call her insurance company and try to get it taken care of before she got back.

Aria screamed with excitement and I smiled. This, this is what life was all about. I could've given her crap about just having met the guy and how crazy she was acting, but I didn't. For once, I could let go of the stress from the past week and let Aria's happiness wash over me. Life was good.

KISS & MAKEUP

BOOK 2

Beauty Secrets Series

FREE PREVIEW

"*B*ut is it too white?" Aria stared at herself in the floor-length mirror.

I glanced up from my phone, totally over this whole wedding-dress business. What was supposed to be a thirty-minute dress fitting had turned into a three-hour ordeal. Never mind the fact that it was also my birthday and Aria had completely forgotten it. Add that to the fact that she had tried on dozens of gowns before settling on this one two months ago; and now at her final fitting, she was having second thoughts? You could see my annoyance.

The seamstress, Aria's cousin, and the other bridesmaid —Christina—were all doing their best to reassure her. "Too white? Impossible. You look gorgeous," Christina said. She walked around Aria, fluffing and primping the dress. Christina was a perfectionist and she liked everything just so, including her nude-colored manicure and her intricate hair braids. I tried to ignore her, which was my general MO when it came to Christina. She always thought she was right. Always has.

"Simply beautiful," the seamstress said.

I sided with Aria. One: she hated wearing white. In fact, Aria gravitated toward brighter colors. Red was more her style. And two: the fit was all wrong. Don't get me wrong, the high-necked beaded lace gown was gorgeous, but it just wasn't Aria. I would've told her all this the first time around but, well, I wasn't there. I had been so busy expanding my beauty business that I hadn't had much time to help Aria plan her wedding. No matter. It seemed Christina was stepping up and filling that role, even if she was only a bridesmaid again. A fact that I think she mentioned just twice today. An improvement.

"Girl, what do you think?" Aria looked over at me for approval.

Crud. She knew I couldn't lie to her, but her wedding was only a week away. As in, she had exactly six days until she'd become Mrs. Vincent Delgado. She didn't have much time to order a new custom gown.

"Sorry." I put down my phone. "I was just texting Mrs. DeVine. I told her about that rental space. Remember the one I told you about on Main? I think it's perfect, and she agrees. Gotta talk a few more business details with her later in the week."

Mrs. DeVine was the investment backer for my new beauty business. I had managed to fund the initial research and product run, but that was about as far as my ex's engagement ring had gotten me. Without Mrs. DeVine's support, my business would've been operated out of my apartment for the foreseeable future. I was incredibly lucky to have her on board, but that also meant needing to run things by her and stay in her good graces, which also meant attending the social events she hosted once a month. These gatherings were basically a giant cocktail party for the rich and famous of Savannah, with a little business networking thrown in. The next one was this upcoming Wednesday and I promised her I'd be there, even if I'd rather be at home binge watching Netflix.

"Is that a hive?" I took a closer look at my bestie's face. Her usual warm skin tone was turning into a blotchy mess. "Girl, you gotta calm down. You know you could wear a trash bag and Vince would still marry you." True story. The man adored her. Plus, he was filthy rich, which somehow made it even more exciting. He bought islands and fancy cars the way some people bought shoes or scratch-off lottery tickets. (Hey, don't judge.)

"You're right." Aria took a deep breath.

I stood up from the cream-colored couch. "Listen, I'd love to continue our little party, but I have a hot date and a cake with my name on it waiting for me."

It was Seaside Days. The annual kick-off-the-summer festival Port Haven was known for. Finn was going to meet me there to celebrate my birthday and watch the bake-off action. Mrs. Birdie Jackson, aka Mrs. J., the town gossip queen and my surrogate nana, was after the championship title and the competition was fierce. I wouldn't miss it for the world, even if she didn't also have a birthday cake waiting for me. Not to mention the fact there were plenty of free samples to go around too. If I was lucky, maybe even a corn dog. Carnival eats should be their own food group.

"But, we're not done yet," Christina insisted, referencing the list on her ever-present clipboard.

"Oh, but you know me and cake," I said with a devilish smile.

"Oh, girl, I'm so sorry." Aria turned awkwardly to step down from the carpeted pedestal. The fabric twisted around her feet. I went to her instead. "I can't believe I totally forgot. Happy birthday!"

"It's okay, girl. You're a bit of a hot mess right now, but I still love you. I do have to go, though. Mrs. J. made my favorite." No need to elaborate. Everyone knew my favorite was Mrs. J.'s famous chocolate cake with its ooey-gooey filling and warm chocolate sauce on top. My mouth tingled in anticipation of the sugar. I may have even drooled.

"Mind if I come with?" Christina asked.

"Wha-? Uh, I guess not." What happened to not being done yet? I guess cake had the same effect on Christina.

"She's baking the wedding cake, right?" Christina asked. That she was. Aria had wanted to go with some vegan confection, but I talked her out of that nonsense. "Well, as Aria's unofficial wedding planner, I think I should taste it, to make sure it's good enough for our bride-to-be." Christina said the last part all sing song-y. *Oh brother.*

Aria shrugged her bare shoulders. "Just give me five minutes. I want to talk to the seamstress about our dresses and then I'll be ready."

Our dresses were a cranberry-satin number. Completely ugly, also Christina's doing.

"Okay, five minutes," I said. Maybe four and a half and then I was out of there.

MY MOM CALLED for the third time that day on the drive downtown.

"Ziva dear, you didn't answer me. Is Finn coming tomorrow?" Ugh, why wouldn't she just drop it? No way was I inviting Finn over to dinner at my parents. Birthday dinner implied a certain level of relationship status that I was trying to avoid. I had already learned that lesson and kept Finn a safe distance from my heart.

"Sorry, Mom. Not happening. He's taking off tomorrow for work. But I'll pass the invite on." *Liar, liar pants on fire.* But what was I going to say? My mother expected nothing less. She put the P in proper, which wasn't a surprise seeing that her mom and Mrs. J. had been best friends. Those ladies had spent a lifetime gathering dirt on everyone. The secrets those two must've known… My mom made sure none of them were about her.

I dropped the thought as we caught up to traffic. Seaside Days was the festival of the year for Port Haven. This event turned our small seaside town into a happening hot spot.

The high school parking lot transformed into a carnival, Main Street was packed with sidewalk sales and street vendors, and the ocean-front park pavilion morphed into ground zero. This weekend's events featured an airshow, farmers market, country-music concert, and of course, fireworks. If you were a small-business owner, you cherished Seaside Days more than Christmas. I was planning on using the extra publicity to launch my own personal business—Serenity Now. I was introducing the spa line first as to not compete with my Beauty Secrets clientele. Privately, I already had friends raving about and reviewing my product line, but this weekend was going to be my grand public debut before opening my storefront next month (hopefully!). Thanks to the added investment of Mrs. DeVine, my business was blooming faster than I could have ever imagined. I needed everything to be perfect this weekend.

Parking, of course, was a nightmare, which is why I agreed to meet Finn at the marina where he worked, and we'd walk down together. I parked my cute little pickup next to his real truck on the scorched grass next to Murphy's Bait and Tackle. The spot had become my unofficial parking space.

Finn made his way down the docks as we turned the corner to search for him. His shirtless state and khaki cargo shorts put a smile on my face. *Happy birthday to me.* Before I met him, I had dubbed him the "shirtless hottie," and the nickname still fit.

Christina smiled at him a little too sweetly. I didn't blame her. He was smokin'.

"Happy birthday, babe," Finn greeted me with a kiss on the cheek. He lingered for just a moment, but it was long enough for me to take in the rugged, sexual scent of motor oil mixed with cologne that was quintessentially him.

"Do you girls want to come up?" Finn's studio apartment was above the bait shop. Thankfully, he had a separate outside entrance. The waterfront views were amazing. The sunrise? Not so much.

"No, that's okay. You run up. We'll wait right here." If Christina hadn't been with us, my answer would have been much, much different. I tempered down my thoughts by reminding myself that the bake off was set to start in forty minutes, and I didn't want to be late. I was sure it was going to be a mouthwatering event. Grand prize was also five thousand dollars, but it wasn't about the cash for Mrs. J. She was all about the bragging rights. If you asked me, she didn't need a title; she was the best baker in Georgia.

FINN WAS BACK DOWN at the docks and ready to go in less than ten minutes. Seriously, how did guys do that? I hadn't introduced Christina yet, so we took a few seconds to get that formality out of the way and then discussed our game plan. As far as Christina was concerned, she was only there to taste the cake and then be on her way. Knowing Christina, she probably had a checklist that she *had* to get back to. That was fine by me. The girl was way more organized than I could've ever hoped to be. Even as kids, she had a love of making lists and she always insisted on being the teacher when we played school. Somehow, I always got detention.

We heard Mrs. J. before we saw her.

"Now you wait just a second, Paulette. I told the committee I was making this cake, and that's exactly what I'm going to do."

Paulette scrutinized the recipe card in her hand. Her

salt-and-pepper hair swept across her face. She wore a silver headband that wasn't doing its job, but it did match the silver sequined blazer she wore. I had no idea how she could stand it. Not the sequins, although that was questionable, but the long sleeves with this heat. It had to be ninety degrees out.

"Well, I'm not even sure this recipe qualifies. It might be one of them copycat ones. You see them on the internet all the time," she said with authority in her voice. "And secret ingredients? Tsk-tsk."

"Copycat my foot! This here is my world-famous chocolate cake, and you know it. I'm not telling you what's in it either!" Mrs. J. had on a bedazzled apron, hot-pink-and-orange leggings, and a lime green shirt. She looked like rainbow sherbet. Crazy, yet somehow still coordinated. "Now, y'all better give me back my recipe and get out of my way. I've got some baking to do."

Paulette didn't move. She stared down Mrs. J. The last time this happened, someone got a pie to the face.

"Just think, next year I'll be a judge and you'll be baking for me!" Mrs. J. said. "Honorary Judge, there's nothing honorary here," she added under her breath. Last year, Paulette won the competition and had been promoted to judge along with her best friend, Suzanne Butterfield, who I saw joining them now. Mrs. J. was still not over it. I didn't think she'd ever be.

"Ha! Over my dead body. You'll NEVER be a judge," Paulette said, puffing out her chest.

"Don't tempt me." Mrs. J. narrowed her eyes and took a fighting stance. My surrogate nana could deliver a threat like a boss. It was inspiring.

"Please, you hardly scare me." But Paulette took a step

back. Suzanne looked behind her. I wondered if she was looking for a pie.

"Ladies, if you please." The town mayor, Mr. Humphrey Potts, hobbled over with his ivory-handled cane and tried to defuse the situation. "We have guests." His head motioned to the gathering crowd, in a nervous sort of way. The women ignored him. If he was smart, he would've just gotten out of the way. Mayor Potts wouldn't get anywhere with those two. This feud had been going on for years. They weren't about to stop. Besides, I never thought of Mayor Potts as an authority figure with his bumbling personality. The title Town Ambassador was more appropriate, which was probably why he was the festival's Grand Marshal every year.

"Admit it, that's why you're not baking this year. Couldn't handle a little competition," Mrs. J. said.

"Oh Birdie, you're pathetic. Must I remind you, *Deep South Cuisine* named my pecan torte Best of the Best," Paulette said.

"That's true, they did," Suzanne said, nodding her head to the gathering crowd.

"Well, whoopty flippin' do. I guess that settles it," Mrs. J. replied, twirling her finger in a circle.

"And you darn well know last year I won fair and square," Paulette insisted.

"If you call having relations with the festival's Grand Marshal fair and square..." Mrs. J. trailed off. Mr. Pott's complexion now matched his red bow tie. Suzanne covered her mouth with her hand and widened her eyes.

"Why you!" Paulette got all huffy. She turned her head to the right and then left in swift desperation, but no pies were in sight.

Mrs. J. smirked. I wasn't sure if I should laugh or be horrified. Finn found it totally amusing. Christina's eyes nearly bulged out of her head. I bet they didn't have drama like this at the country club.

"UGH!" Paulette turned on her heel and marched off, balling up Mrs. J.'s recipe card in her fist and throwing it on the ground. Suzanne threw an evil eye at Mrs. J. and followed Paulette. Mayor Potts trailed after them both, picking the card up and smiling at the crowd as if it had all been part of the show.

"Humph. I'd like to put a little something extra in her cake," Mrs. J. mumbled. I could relate. I had my own frenemy that brought out the worst in me. I tried to keep it in check, because, you know, Karma and all that; but man, sometimes … Justine could irk me like no one else. *Speak of the devil,* I thought, as I saw her making her way through the crowd. She had her dolled-up poodle under one arm and was passing out flyers with the other. I didn't even want to know. I turned my back to her and got Mrs. J.'s attention.

"So, you ready to do this?" I asked her.

"Sug'!" Mrs. J. wrapped me in a giant hug. She smelled like chocolate and peppermint, and I drank it all in. She whispered, "And I see you brought Mr. Hot Pants, too." I gave her a little extra squeeze.

"Hey, this is Christina," I said when we broke free. "She's Aria's cousin. I told her you were making the wedding cake and she wanted to give it a little sample."

"Well, it's no buttercream; but if you ask me, this tastes better." Mrs. J. turned to the table behind her and came back with a bakery box filled with her chocolate cake. I opened the box and took in a big whiff. Forget a plate. Someone needed to get me a fork, stat!

"Happy birthday, sweets."

"Thanks, Mrs. J."

"You enjoy it, now. I got to be getting to work. The show starts in twenty minutes." Mrs. J. scooted us on our way.

We wished her luck and headed toward the makeshift food court, which was basically an open area with plastic tables and chairs, with food vendors outlining the perimeter. I didn't even let them sing "Happy Birthday" to me. We cut into the cake with a plastic knife and I doled out the deliciousness. Any skepticism Christina might have harvested vanished the moment that cake was in her mouth. I could see it in her eyes. Dessert nirvana. I'd be a total liar if I didn't say I would've eaten more than my fair share if Finn and Christina hadn't been there. The cake was that good. But, seeing that I was trying to be a lady (don't laugh) and we couldn't take a cake on the Ferris wheel, I thought it would be nice to give some away. So, I did. Satisfied with the cake, Christina took off, and Finn and I passed out the remaining slices on paper plates to whomever wanted one. Well, everyone except Justine. She tried to snag a piece from Finn (did I mention she was also his psychotic ex-girlfriend? Small world, huh?), but I told her no. And then I smiled.

Finn and I were back in the grandstands and ready to watch the show right when it started. Mrs. J. was cracking eggs, whisking batter, and adding a dash of this and that to her mixing bowls, all the while sporting a beaming smile as if she were on her own cooking show, laughing with the audience and telling stories about this or that. The other two contestants were all business. Wendy Swiss was making a caramel cake, and she looked like a total wreck. Even sitting three rows back, I could see her hands shaking. She was no competition. The other contestant, Mary Dubbs, was making miniature lemon soufflés. Although, I wasn't sure if she was making dessert or running a special op. She had everything from measuring spoons and candy thermometers to a citrus peeler and lemon zester strapped to the utility belt of her cargo pants. She even wore black army boots that looked like she was used to stomping out the competition. *Now, **she** might be a threat.*

Mrs. J. hummed as she worked until WA-WOOM! A small fire ball shot up from Wendy's stovetop. We all jumped back. I instinctively covered my eyebrows. It wouldn't have been the first time they were singed off. I liked to think I was a master at penciling in brows, but thankfully they were safe. We all stared as caramelized liquid bubbled and oozed over the pan and spilled across the cooktop. Wendy stood dumbfounded with a bottle of rum in her hand. Mrs. J. ran over and turned off the gas and pulled the pot from the flame. Military Mary didn't even look over. She was too busy zesting a lemon to death. Wendy burst into tears and ran off the stage, leaving Mrs. J. standing there with a literal hot mess on her hands. Mr. Humphrey arrived a moment later with a fire extinguisher and a roll of paper towels. With the chaos under control, Mrs. J. went back to her station and began whipping up her signature chocolate sauce. She was hilarious, trying to hide exactly what was in it, but I saw that she added a lot of butter and chocolate, and the last ingredient was some type of syrup. It looked like honey. I would've never thought to add that to a chocolate sauce. I'd have loved to ask Mrs. J. about it, but I knew she wouldn't elaborate. Regardless, I would've enjoyed licking that spoon.

When all was said and done, Mrs. J. had turned out a sensational cake. My mouth watered as I knew it tasted just as good. With two minutes to spare, she plated the judges' pieces, gave them one last drizzle of her special chocolate sauce, and turned them in. Military Mary had finished ten minutes earlier and was doing calisthenics on the sidelines.

Wendy Swiss sat in the bleachers, still crying over her disastrous performance.

The judges sat at the front of the stage, analyzing the desserts from every angle, and deliberating in dramatic fashion while the audience waited with bated breath. A couple of middle-school band students were brought on stage to provide entertainment and ease the tension while we waited. Their rendition of *God Bless America* was about as good as you could imagine, and did little to settle the nerves that were dancing in my stomach. I wondered how Mrs. J. was holding up. I looked around to see for myself, but she was nowhere to be found.

Finally, after way too long and one too many musical versus, Mayor Potts was back front and center with a microphone in hand, ready to announce the winner. Mrs. J. popped back in place from wherever she had been, looking poised and ready to accept her award. I saw she was sporting fresh Passion Pout lipstick, a favorite hue of hers, and her apron had been tossed aside. Her confidence was contagious and I beamed at her in anticipation of her victory. I was just waiting to hear her name so I could rush over and congratulate her.

Finn put his hand on my bouncing knee. "Settle down, cowboy," he said, and laughed. I swatted his hand away and shushed him. Mayor Potts was getting ready to speak.

"Should we get to it, then?" The mayor gave a bit of a nervous chuckle. "All right then! The winner of this year's Seaside Days championship bake off is ... drum roll please ... Mary Dubbs!"

Mic drop. The earth quaked in response, and I shivered.

Mary sprung onto stage like it had been a planned part of her workout. She pumped her fists in the air and bounced around the stage as if she had just knocked Mrs. J. out. The enthusiasm was all her own. A few people politely clapped, but anyone who knew Mrs. J. kept silent. I looked for Mrs. J. to see how she was handling the news, and did a double take. She was already rushing the stage. *Sweet sugar!* I leapt into action, but Mrs. J. was already having it out with Paulette before I could reach her.

"You rotten woman! That title is mine!" she shouted.

Paulette couldn't even get a word in.

"I hate you. This is just like you. You lie and you cheat, and I'm so sick of it!"

Mayor Potts stared at the ladies, who were having it out on the stage, horrified. I was pretty shocked too, and I knew how vocal Mrs. J. could be.

"You rigged this. So help me, Paulette. This doesn't end here!" Mrs. J. stormed off before turning and pointing at the mayor. "You too!" she threatened. Mayor Potts looked a little white around the collar. You did not want to be on Mrs. J.'s bad side, especially if you were in politics. If anyone could air someone's dirty laundry, it was Mrs. J. I didn't dare go after her. She needed to cool down about a thousand degrees before I'd touch her.

Mayor Potts gave another nervous laugh into the microphone. "Let's hear it once again for Mary! That was some dessert." He clapped. Mary clapped. The rest of the crowd was silent. *Awkward.*

I walked back off the stage and rejoined Finn. He looked at me with a huge grin. "Well, that was fun. Funnel cake?"

"You're terrible."

"What?" Finn looked all innocent. "C'mon, admit it. That was awesome. I bet someone posts it online." I really, really hoped they didn't, but Finn was probably right. I was sure it would go viral.

I should probably have felt like puking after all the junk I ate and carnival rides we rode. Funnel cakes, corn dogs, cotton candy, French fries, and that's only the stuff I remembered. Finn was a ride warrior. If it spun, swung, or dropped, he was all about it. I'd bet he'd go crazy at a real amusement park. Something to keep in mind. My head was still spinning.

The afternoon had finally ended and now it was time for my favorite part: fireworks. My birthday seemed to always be during Seaside Days. When I was little, I believed my dad when he said the fireworks were just for me. We had swung back by Finn's apartment for a blanket and a few drinks before heading down to the beach to claim our spot. The fireworks were launched off a barge straight in front of us. We couldn't have asked for a better view.

With the carnival behind us and the ocean in front, it was super romantic. My stomach churned again, only this time it had nothing to do with the carnival. *Maybe we should've made this a group thing.* Aria and Vince would've probably joined us. I could've still given her a call. I was a second away from texting Aria and seeing what she was up to, when Finn brought me back to the present. "Here. Happy birthday." He took a jewelry box out of his cargo shorts pocket.

Oh heck no. There better not be anything of the diamond variety in that little box. We hadn't been dating for that long. My heart pounded and I thought I'd pass out right then and there.

I must've looked terrified because Finn said, "Chill out, it's nothing like that. I know you."

I gave the phoniest laugh ever. Good grief, I was pathetic. I fumbled with the box and opened it. Inside was a beautiful silver charm bracelet with three charms: a high heel, a lipstick, and a champagne flute. He did know me, and well. "Finn, seriously, this is awesome. I love it." I kissed him full on the mouth in a beautiful public display of affection.

Finn rummaged in our little cooler and brought out a mini bottle of champagne. "I forgot the cups."

"That's okay." I was never one to turn down a little bubbly, and I could sure use a drink after my little freak out back there.

He popped the cork and handed me the bottle.

"Cheers, birthday girl. I have a feeling this year's going to be great."

"Me too." This *was* going to be the year. I had big dreams.

"So, tomorrow?" I asked.

"Yeah, sorry about that. Did you want me to see if someone else can take it?"

An offshore fishing trip had just been booked and Finn was set to take them out through the week. He had recently taken over the charter business for Mr. Murphy, and his trips had quickly built a following, thanks to his mad social media skills and his Instagram followers.

"No, it's cool. Seriously. Besides, you hate weddings as much as I do." With Finn out of town, there was no pressure for him to be my date. Bonus.

"I didn't say that. What I said was I didn't like them. You however, have serious wedding issues." *So very true.* This, of course, might have something to do with the fact that my ex-fiancé cheated on me two weeks before our wedding. Not going to lie, I still wasn't over it. Finn only knew part of the story, which was the way I planned on keeping it.

"Anyway, don't worry about the wedding. Not only that,

but I have a bunch of work stuff going on. I'm sure the week will fly by."

"Just a girl boss."

"Building her empire," I said with a smile.

With a champagne bottle in hand and a gorgeous bracelet on my wrist, I leaned back, oohing and ahhing as the fireworks lit up the night sky. Did I know how to celebrate my birthday, or what? My favorite fireworks were the gold sparkly ones that popped and fizzed like giant Rice Krispies. Finn was all about the weeping willow ones that cascaded down the sky until dipping into the ocean. He pointed them out every single time, as if I could miss seeing them. I laughed at his innocence. The speakers on the grandstand played a mixture of eighties tunes and Americana music in sync with the blasts. It was a display of patriotism at its finest. With every explosion, the sand shook a little bit and the sensation reverberated in my chest. I loved it.

THIRTY MINUTES LATER, the show was wrapping up. Blast after blast shot off from the barge in front. It almost looked like the platform was on fire with how quickly the shells were being launched. When the celebration ended, the entire beach and grandstands area erupted in cheers. I could already hear people saying how great the show was, comparing it to previous years. So far, everyone thought the town had done a fabulous job. We waited a few minutes while everyone seemed to make a mad dash, gathering their kids and gear, to beat traffic. Thankfully, we wouldn't be dealing with that mess.

"You about ready to head back?" I asked a few minutes

later. I had only brought one of Finn's sweatshirts to throw over my cutoffs, and the night air had cooled several degrees.

"Yeah, let's go. I may or may not have a surprise waiting for you." Finn reached for my hand and brought it up to his lips for a kiss. Surprises weren't really my thing, but I had a feeling I'd love whatever Finn had in store.

"Beach or boardwalk?" he asked.

"Beach. Less crowded." Most of the crowd had thinned out except for the few bonfires that had popped up, and the kids who ran around on the beach with sparklers in hand.

I started to ask Finn more about his planned charter. "So, where are you going exactly?"

"Making a run from Savannah to St. Augustine with a couple of island stops along the way. It's basically the best vacation ever."

Ha, I doubted that. In my opinion, the best vacation involved the beach, a fruity cocktail, and my bikini. I turned my head and started to tell him so when I tripped over something and went flying face-first in the sand. My hands cushioned the blow, but I still took in a mouthful of grit.

"Hey, you okay?" Finn had dropped the cooler and blanket and rushed to my side.

"What the heck?" I rolled over and Finn gave me a hand up. I whipped the sand off my clothes and face, and tried to spit out the remnants in my mouth as ladylike as possible; but there was no proper way to do this, I discovered. At least I didn't get any in my eyes.

I looked behind me in the darkness to try and see what I had tripped over. "Sweet sugar!" I jumped back. A human foot was sticking out of the sand. Finn froze next to me and I knew he saw it too.

"Tell me this wasn't my birthday surprise," I said.

"Not even close."

I wish I could say this was the first dead body we'd found together. This time, I let him call the cops.

KISS & MAKEUP

A wedding, a feud, and a dead body. What could go wrong?

Ziva Diaz was really looking forward to this week. Her best friend's getting married and her new beauty line is launching. But stumbling over a dead body on the beach trips her up in more ways than one. Her beauty client, Mrs. Birdie Jackson, is charged with the murder and she asks Ziva to clear her name. Ziva believes that Mrs. J. would never murder anyone, too bad she's the only one. As Ziva sets out to solve the mystery someone else sets out to ruin her reputation and her friend's wedding.

Can Ziva solve the case and serve up some just desserts? Or will her investigation fall flatter than a wedding soufflé?

Now Available!

A RING TO DIE FOR

FREE Beauty Secrets Short Story

Ziva's bestie has been framed for robbing a jewelry store and it's up to her to crack the case. The situation quickly turns deadly and suddenly a robbery is small potatoes compared to what Ziva uncovers.

Dive in to the world of Beauty Secrets in this fast-paced, whodunit mystery.

Visit stephaniedamore.com to download it today!

ABOUT THE AUTHOR

Stephanie Damore is a mystery author who loves all things girlie with a dollop of danger. Her books feature fearless females, a little bit of love, a few laughs, and a whole lot of whodunit. She hopes her books keep you guessing and laughing all the way until the end.

For new releases and giveaways, visit me at:
www.stephaniedamore.com
steph.damore@gmail.com

Made in the USA
Middletown, DE
01 May 2018